PAWS FOR THOUGHT

By the same author
Charlie Coppins

PAWS FOR THOUGHT

Neville Crine

Illustrated by
Liz Graham-Yooll

COLLINS

William Collins Sons & Co Ltd
London · Glasgow · Sydney · Auckland
Toronto · Johannesburg

First published 1990
© text Neville McAuslan-Crine 1990
© illustrations Liz Graham-Yooll 1990

A CIP catalogue record for this book is
available from the British Library.

ISBN 0 00 195488-1

Printed and bound in Great Britain
by Hartnolls, Bodmin, Cornwall

For Polly and The Others

Chapter One

The first morning back at school after Christmas, Charlie's mum stayed home because her friend was coming, so she got Charlie his breakfast. He was just mopping up his bean juice when Wayne Nuttley turned up. If Nuttley came on his own bike, he propped it up against the chicken house. If it was on Pearson's delivery bike, he let it go with a crash, just where he got off. He came in through with a packet of crumpets in his hand.

"Leftovers," he said. "Someone ordered too many."

"Charlie'll stick them under the grill for you," Charlie's mum said. "Well go on then, Charlie. If you want them you can cook them. There's a bit of marge in the fridge if it hasn't all gone." Then she let go a yawn from behind her mug. "I know what I want . . . I want a nice long holiday."

"I told you my idea for a holiday," Charlie called over from the cooker.

"What was that then?"

"That holiday I thought up for me and Dad. Where we'd stay in the old bus on the beach with surf boards on the roof and straw umbrellas up over our dinner table on the beach. You said it'd be dead boring."

"I'd like one like that," Wayne put in. "All that surfing and swimming. I reckon I'd end up that good they'd come round and pay me a fortune just to do a telly advert."

Charlie's mum put her mug down. "Too much like hard work, all that," she said. "My idea's better. I want a real smart hotel where everything's done for you, right down to someone else turning on your bath taps for you. I'll have a taxi to take me round all the shows, waiters to bring me my dinner, and I'll have breakfast in bed. Every morning for a month. Who wants to spend their holiday squashed up inside some old bus?"

Charlie came over with the crumpets. "If anything sounds dead boring, that does," he said. "It doesn't sound like it'd give us that much time in the sunshine."

Charlie's mum coughed. "Us?" she said. "And who said you were coming? This is my dream holiday, my love, my very own dream holiday. People don't drag their kids round with them while they're having their dream holiday. Not if they've got any sense they don't. Anyway, all that sun sends you wrinkly."

"Dad reckoned my idea was all right," Charlie answered. "Why not have your taxi-ride holiday first, and then you could come on out and join

8

me and Dad on the beach when it was all over. There's straw umbrellas for people going wrinkly."

Charlie's mum reached for her bag. "Well it's all silly dreams, isn't it. Something you and your father are good at, fancy holidays. Just you be grateful there's money enough for your next meal. Here it is. Oh, and I'm helping out at the pub tonight, so I'll be late back. I'll have my supper there I expect. Nice to see you, Wayne."

Charlie's house was one of the old railway cottages up the line, past where the crossing gates used to let the train cross the road. His house was the end one. All the rest were boarded up. They had lots of space for all sorts of things up there,

9

Charlie and his dad, because they'd moved the fence back so that their chickens could stretch their legs and trot round the old railway car park as well. Charlie's dad had taken off the shutters round the back of their next door house, so he could use the extra space. He'd made a workshop and all sorts in there, but nobody else was meant to know that.

Charlie looked just like his dad. His hair was all black and spikey and he had a sort of pale, boiled look, just like he'd been put through the wash. His clothes looked just the same. All the blue had been boiled out of his jeans, and they'd shrunk that much they stopped short way above

his socks. His pullover had gone the same way, even though he tried to pull the sleeves down. He'd pulled them so much, they'd come apart at the elbows and his shirt showed through. If it bothered Charlie he never said.

His mum was quite different. She worked at the hairdressers' in Castlebury, and she went off every day in a special car all dressed up like she was going to a party. She worked long hours, because some nights she got back so late Charlie was already up in bed.

She left him his supper, of course, that or the chip van money on the window sill. Charlie didn't seem to mind getting his supper on his own once his dad had gone off. If he had to go down to the chip van, he sat out on the grass and ate his Fatty Scratchings straight off, before they got cold. If it was wet he took them back home and had them by the telly. There weren't many people who could say they lived like Charlie.

Charlie's dad was off working somewhere else. He had a van he drove around in, doing odd jobs and all sorts. He'd been running his do-it-yourself rocking horse business before he went away. He never had a market stall or anything like that. All he did was back his van up on the pavement in Castlebury and open the back doors. He used to put a big shining rocking horse out on the pavement so that people would know what their construction kits would look like when they finished, and sing out to people walking past that he had the answer to that special Christmas present. All they had to do was buy the kit and fix the parts together and they'd have a great big rocking horse just like the one on the pavement.

He never told anyone that they were just buying odd bits of wood, all done up inside plastic bags Farmer Braddon used for his fertilizer. By the time they got home and found out they had to cut it all to shape for themselves, he had shut his van doors and gone.

They tracked him down, though. A whole bus load of unhappy woodworkers turned up at Charlie's house one night and brought Sergeant Edgely with them. Charlie's dad had to go off to Castlebury police station so he could sort it all out, and that was the last time he'd been home. He must have packed his business up straight after that and gone off to work somewhere else.

Long Tussocks School. Headmistress Mrs E. Trugg. Keys at the Vicarage, was on the opposite side of the green to Pearson's Stores, with the Lime Kiln pub on one side and the church on the other. Everybody went there, from the moment they got left by their mums down at the grass end with Miss Tinsdale, right to when they got to the top end with Mrs Trugg.

Nobody minded it down in the littles. They

had a sandpit and a washing line for their dolls'
clothes and a piano of their own for when they
had singing. Mrs Trugg's lot at the top had a good
life too. They went over the wall into Farmer
Braddon's for rural science and they kept the telly
in their room. Anybody else who wanted it had
to knock and ask and then wheel it back down
the corridor.

Charlie Coppins and Wayne Nuttley were in
Mr Greysock's class. Mr Greysock took the
middles. In the middles it was rough. No one in
Mr Greysock's class got so much as a glimpse of
a sandpit or a chance of slipping over Farmer
Braddon's wall to wash the pig pens. Nobody
ever told the littles down with Miss Tinsdale that
one day they'd have to leave off singing all day
and frying plastic eggs on wooden cookers and
move up to Mr Greysock's middles. People
reckoned it was better they didn't know.

Nobody liked going back after Christmas. Last
time they'd been in school it had all been like
some blazing art gallery, what with the panto-
mime scenery propped up all over the place and
people wandering round practising their parts. Mr
Greysock spent all his time actually being kind to
people just in case they didn't come back on the
night when everyone in Long Tussocks came to
see the show.

Only two weeks later, and everything was back

to normal, just like nothing special had happened. All the pictures were off the walls because Mr Flint had been round with his bucket and washed the bricks with Farmer Braddon's pig disinfectant. Some of the drawing pins in the ceiling stayed all year round with bits of decoration still stuck to them, but everything else was whipped away in case the idea got around that Christmas lasted for ever.

Everybody got shoved outside at playtimes. The boys kicked the football round and the girls hung about doing handstands and playing two-ball and all sorts under the staffroom window. Coppins and his lot never joined in with any of it. They had a special place of their own up against the wall of the boys' toilets, or over by the kitchen fan hole if it was cold. If it wasn't that wet, they sat on the ground. Nuttley always lay flat along the ground with just his head up the wall. Colin Dibble usually sat on a book in case the cold got up to his chest. It was odd really. Nobody else ever tried to take over Charlie's corner.

Wayne Nuttley started up the moment they got out to play. "You're just all mouth, you are, Coppins," he said, once he'd propped himself up against the toilet wall. "You haven't got a dog for a start, and if you had, the welfare man would have been round and taken it off you for cruelty

to dumb animals. Look at all those skinny chickens you've got up there. If they weren't designed with scratchy feet they'd never get a bite to eat right through their lives."

He was right really. When Charlie's dad had been home, he and Charlie used to drive round the lanes in their van collecting up stray chickens. Charlie's dad used to say he was saving them from getting run over, but he never stopped long enough to ask what anyone else thought. He ended up with so many, he couldn't afford to feed them all, so he let them run round the old railway car-park to scratch around for themselves.

"It's not chickens I'm on about, nut-case," Charlie snorted back. "Can't you tell the difference between a chicken and a racing dog? Dogs are where the real money is. If I had a dog, I'd clean up on every race going. I'd train it to run that fast it'd be in every race in the country. Good way to live that."

Colin Dibble joined in. "Our Tricksy's won her class three years running now. She's been in the Top Terrier Class ever since we put her in."

"Who said anything about little bog-rat terriers?" said Charlie. "It's real dogs we're talking about, Dibble, not squeaky little guinea pigs. Just think about it. There's going to be some mighty powerful runners in the Big Dog Handicap on Saturday. That's where you'll see real dog-power. All the other races will be nothing compared with that one. Fifty pounds for the winner. If I had a dog big enough, that's the race he'd be in."

"I'm helping my dad in the measuring compound," Wayne said.

"My mum's letting me be Tricksy's handler," Colin Dibble put in. "I can hold her at the start of her race, but my mum said she'll be the one going up for the prize."

"Your mingy little ferret's not won yet, dimmo," Charlie said. "You'd better not let it get near the Big Dog line-up, or they'll eat it for their tea." The whistle went. "Come on, it's hymn practice. I'm doing the books."

Charlie was still looking thoughtful, even while

he was dishing the books out. Most times, he shuffled them round so he got a shiny one for himself, but his mind was so far away on other things he ended up having to share a really tatty one with Biddy Perkins.

Now Biddy Perkins was one of the dimmest dimmos of all time, so anyone letting himself end up sharing a hymn book with someone like her must have had something pretty heavy on his mind. Biddy was still on Radiant Way Book One from when she was in Miss Tinsdale's. Mr Greysock gave her the register monitor's job so she could learn her way round school, but she still managed to get lost, even though she'd been doing it for years. That's how dim Perkins was. Oddly enough, Charlie just sang his hymn at the top of his voice like he always did. He couldn't have noticed who his partner was.

Most days when it came up to dinner time, everybody had to go on working till the bell went, but when it was hymn practice in the hall the dinner ladies always brought things to a stop by coming in at the back and smacking the tables about. Wayne was one of the first people out, but when he looked round for Charlie he couldn't find him. In the end he went back inside to see where he'd got to.

Charlie was still in the hall, talking to Biddy Perkins of all people.

"You all right, Charlie?" Wayne asked.

Charlie just nodded and let Biddy slide off into the corridor. "Just fixing things for Saturday," he said, all airy. "If you're helping your dad in the measuring compound, you'd better be ready with your tape measure for something pretty special."

"Just what are you up to, Coppins?" Wayne said, not one bit impressed by Charlie being all mysterious. "If you want us to measure your big head, then we can't do it. There isn't a tape measure long enough."

Charlie jumped straight in at that and thumped Wayne a dead leg. "Don't you be so cocky, nutcase," he said, skipping off backwards in case Wayne thumped him one back. "You're only helping measure dogs' legs, so you're nothing special. Just you wait till Saturday. You'll see. You'll come creeping round soon enough for a sniff of my prize money. And a sniff's just about all you're going to get."

Wayne walked off, trying to keep up straight so Charlie couldn't see one of his legs wasn't working.

"There'll be enough for you as well if you want," Charlie called after him. "You can come on that holiday me and my dad's having. That's if you're not frightened of going wrinkly."

18

Chapter Two

Most mornings Charlie went into school long before anybody else because he helped Mr Flint do the chairs. But on the second day back there wasn't a sign of him, even after the whistle had gone.

Charlie had reasons of his own, of course, for helping Mr Flint. It wasn't because he enjoyed dragging furniture around, that was certain. Charlie came in so he could sit inside in the warm, drinking tea out of Mr Flint's flask in the caretaker's hole next to the sick room, while everybody else was hanging round outside in the cold.

Nuttley was late that morning as well. They hadn't turned up even while Mr Greysock was calling the register. Mr Greysock had got as far as Elsie Carpenter when Charlie came gasping in from the corridor, just in time to save getting marked absent. It didn't surprise anyone when Nuttley came staggering in only a minute behind him.

"Sorry, Sir," Charlie whispered, trying to wipe his nose and smile all friendly at the same time. "Nobody said you were starting early." He was really puffing for his breath. "We were up watching the fire. Didn't notice the time had gone on."

Mr Greysock put his eyebrows up like he wasn't that impressed. "The rest of us don't get all that much time to sit by our fires in the mornings," he said, all lofty. "We just do boring things like getting in to school on time. And why all this fire-watching, might I ask? I thought you spent all your time watching the telly."

Charlie frowned. "It was a proper fire, honest it was. There's a lorry turned over up Tussocks Cross. The fire engine's still there." He turned round to make sure Wayne Nuttley was nodding.

"Why don't we all go up there and take a look?" Andy Timms called out from the back. "We could call it a nature ramble. Mrs Trugg wouldn't mind."

Mr Greysock put on his doesn't-it-take-your-breath-away look, like his life was becoming more unbelievable every minute.

"And a Happy New Year to you too, Andrew Timms," he said. "You've only just finished two whole weeks wandering round the great outdoors, and now you're putting in for extra time! We aren't going anywhere. Charlie, you and Wayne can stay out here and tell us all about it. There's no assembly so we've got a little time in hand. Five minutes, no more."

Everybody settled back, of course. It didn't

happen that often, Charlie Coppins and Wayne Nuttley getting called upon to tell a story.

"There was this gert pile of smoke," Charlie began. He got it out so fast he had to stop and swallow. Then he pulled his jeans up as far as they would go in case they slid down while he was talking. "I saw it when I was out feeding the chickens. I thought it was old – er Farmer Braddon burning up car tyres and all that, but it was in the wrong place."

"I saw it while I was doing the papers," Nuttley put in. "We went up on the bikes."

Charlie took over again. "There was this lorry right over on its side with all its underneath showing – and flames and smoke all over the place, really burning." He turned so Wayne could say so too.

"When we got there the firemen were still pulling their hoses off the fire engine," Wayne said. "Some of them had to trot off down the road and spray where the petrol had gone."

"The road got so hot it melted," Charlie put in. "There was tar and stuff running down into the ditch. I got some of it on my tyres."

"So did I," said Wayne.

"They just weren't winning with the water hose," Charlie went on, "so they started up their foam gun. It looked just like one of them guns they have on the top of submarines. It really worked. There was tons of it blowing all round the place. They were pumping it round like a knock-out show. There wasn't much left after that."

"Hadn't they brought up enough foam with them?" Mr Greysock asked from the back.

Charlie put on his patient voice. "There wasn't much left of the lorry, I meant," he said slowly.

"Its tyres went on burning longest," Wayne said.

"Was anyone hurt?" Mr Greysock seemed really interested. "What about the lorry driver. Was he all right?"

"The ambulance came, but it didn't take anybody away," Wayne answered. "The driver was sitting on the gate on the other side of the road, watching it all. Sergeant Edgely went over and had a word, but I don't know what he said."

"They poked round in the rubbish and all that, once the flames were just smoke," Charlie said, "but they didn't find anything". He sounded disappointed. "It must have been empty."

"Well, did you find out what had happened?" Mr Greysock asked.

"I went up to talk to the bloke on top of the fire engine squirting foam," Charlie said. "I climbed up behind him, but he jumped that wild when I shouted in his ear he nearly fell off. He said he'd fill me up with foam too if I didn't get

22

down off his engine. I didn't bother after that."

"Sergeant Edgely was talking on his radio," Wayne said. "He was telling the police station that the lorry skidded on a corner and turned over. He said the petrol must have leaked out and caught fire while the driver was off looking for a phone box."

"He must have felt sick when he got back and saw his lorry on fire," Charlie said. "He looked dead miserable sitting up there on that gate. They might make him pay for a new lorry."

As it was, Charlie's moment of glory only lasted till playtime. Sergeant Edgely came into school to bring the football back he'd borrowed for their match on Saturday and he told Mr Greystock all about it. When everybody got back in after play, Mr Greysock was full of it, just like he'd been off to a private conference.

"That fire of yours, Charlie and Wayne," he called over. "I've had the story from the police. It was a truck from a wildlife park somewhere. It only had one poor creature in the back. That was the only casualty."

It made it sound like Charlie had made his story bigger than it really was, saying it all short like that. Charlie didn't let it show. He just nodded like he'd expected it.

It was painting in the afternoon. Mr Greysock always got people doing art work early in the term just so he could get something up on the wall and cover over Mr Flint's clean bricks. Everybody had to choose something from Charlie's story about the fire up at Tussocks Cross. The best ones could come out and talk about their pictures. Most people did flames and fire engines and smoke and all that, but Charlie's was different. Charlie's picture was a man sitting on a gate looking really sad while he smoked his cigarette.

"That's the lorry driver," Charlie said when Mr Greysock asked him about it. "All that firemen lot were joking and skipping about like they were just having a nice day in the sunshine. Nobody bothered to go over and talk to him. He just sat

24

there and watched, all by himself. That's my picture."

By the end of the week, everybody had found something else to talk about. It was the Great Annual Dog Race. Farmer Braddon always opened his top field for the races because it was the only one not under water. Most years it was just a cow field in the summer and a lambing field in the spring, but last year he'd ploughed it up to grow cattle feed and all sorts were still growing in it, left behind by the cutter. There were old brussel sprout plants and thistles still standing there like dead trees. If any of the runners couldn't hop over them they'd have to find a way round if they wanted a medal to take home.

Colin Dibble came skipping up to the measuring compound looking for Wayne Nuttley. It was certainly busy up there. Wayne and his dad were measuring dogs' back legs to make sure which class they got put in. Wayne was wearing his official armband on his anorak sleeve, so he wasn't much interested in ordinary people.

Colin shoved through the crowd to the fence. "Seen Charlie?" he asked Wayne.

"Who?"

"Charlie."

"Charlie Coppins?"

"Yeah."

"No."

Dibble was just about to say something else when he stopped and pointed towards the entrance gate. "There he is. Well, look at that. He's got Meatloaf."

It would have been better if he'd said it was Meatloaf who'd got Charlie. As soon as Meatloaf heard his name yelled out by Colin Dibble, he came trotting over, dragging Charlie with him.

"Just what are doing, Coppins?" Wayne said. "Old man Braddon said he's going to put a bullet through that thing if he ever sees it on his grass again. This is a dog race anyway. They don't take kangaroos crossed with hippos."

"You've got to measure his legs," Charlie said. "I'm putting him in for the Big Dog Handicap."

"I'm not going near him," Wayne answered. "He eats people, he does." He stepped back respectfully. "Isn't he just dead ugly?"

Meatloaf wasn't even interestingly ugly. He was just big and dangerous. Mr Perkins always told people he'd bought him from a real smart kennels out the other side of Castlebury, but everyone reckoned that the smart kennels had paid Mr Perkins to take him off their hands. He was a good cow dog though. All he had to do was let go one of his growls and the whole herd skipped off as though their lives depended on it, which was quite possibly true.

All the races in the Great Annual Dog Race were the same, except that the dogs got bigger each time. The owners had to line their pets up at the top of the field and hang on till Mr Flint came along and gave the word. Most normal dogs wouldn't have bothered to run anywhere, seeing there was nothing to chase except old brussel sprout plants, but they changed their minds once Mr Flint brought the fox along. It was only an empty fox skin stuffed with chicken feathers, but it fooled the dogs. Once it had passed by, the smell got them jumping about so keen they just about pulled their owners' arms off.

Mr Flint's interestingly smelly object was tied to a piece of string stretching all the way down to the bottom of the field at the winning post. Once Mr Flint fired his gun, the pulling-in team down at the bottom jumped to the handles of their winding-in wheel and wound in the string just as fast as their arms could turn it. Up jumped the fox, skipping away down the track through the old cabbages, like it was dancing off into the sunshine for its holidays.

The pulling-in team never saw much of the race. They had a pretend haystack built round them so the dogs couldn't see what they were up to. The only things the dogs knew was that the fox always got down to the end of the field before they did. It just nipped into the haystack through a little trapdoor, and all the snarling and barking in the world never made it come out again. Year after year, the same dogs came back to chase that fox, but they never worked out what was really happening.

Because it was so special, the Big Dog Handicap was the last event. Charlie came round to the measuring compound to find Wayne and Colin.

"Mr Flint said I can have helpers up at the start," he said. "You lot can come up and lend a hand if you want."

"So we can have our arms pulled off too?" Wayne said. "Come on then. If there's any chance that savage great heap might get a sniff of the prize money, we ought to get a share."

There were all sorts up along that starting line, massive hunting dogs, dribbling guard dogs, great, long hairy things and huge, fat woolly ones, all leaping and barking like they hadn't had a meal for a week. Meatloaf didn't know where to show his teeth next.

This was the big event. All the spectators went quiet. The music in the tea tent got turned off. Mr Flint picked up his shouting trumpet and called everyone to order before he walked along with his fox skin, just in case someone let go and he had to run for his life. Then he stepped to one side.

"Are you all a-ready then, me lads?" he called.

What with all the yowling and howling from the runners and the things their owners were saying to them, it wasn't too easy to hear.

"And are you all a-steady?"

"Then. Go."

And just about everything happened. Up leapt the fox and scampered off down the field. Away thundered the runners. Meatloaf took off that fast Charlie felt his fingers sizzle. In one little second, the starting line was empty.

But then something else happened. Some people said afterwards they'd seen it coming, but really it took everybody by surprise.

It might have been the pulling-in team not winding in the fox quick enough. Perhaps they hadn't worked out that this particular set of customers all had much longer legs than any of the others. Perhaps they'd all been cooped up inside a stuffy haystack for too long, just winding in that smelly bundle and stumbling round over empty beer cans since dinner time. Nobody had time to work it out, because in ten long bounds, Meatloaf caught the fox.

Meatloaf was quite used to catching foxes, of course, so it wasn't much of a surprise for him when he felt his teeth close round this one. What

must have been a surprise for him was that this
one didn't stop and ask him to take his teeth back
out again, like all the others did. This one kept
going.

The pulling-in team must have wondered why
their fox had got so heavy, but they didn't give
up. Meatloaf's only way of stopping was to spread
his legs out and try to get a grip on the ground,
but since his next meal was clearly still inclined to
keep travelling, all he could do was go with it.

If the men on the winding machine had seen
Meatloaf coming at them down the field like he
was slicing a new road through the brussel
sprouts, they would have got out sooner.

The little trapdoor in the haystack was only
wide enough for Mr Flint's fox, but in came the

fox and Meatloaf, bringing most of the haystack with them.

It was like someone had blown it up. Men came skipping and stumbling out through the walls, and all the runners came romping in for a party. For the first time in their lives, the fox was still in sight and up for grabs.

After that, it was anyone's fight. They came in from all sides, little dogs from under tea-tables, dogs out through car windows, every racing competitor with time to spare. One dog came in from the lane that didn't even have a ticket!

There wasn't a prize. All the judges ended up in the First Aid tent with the pulling-in team. Mr Bastable announced that the Big Dog Handicap Cup would have to be saved till next year because every runner had come in at the same time.

They all went looking for Charlie Coppins, though. The ones who couldn't walk sent their friends.

Nobody else had gone to all the trouble of borrowing a dog so they could get first prize, and Meatloaf really did get in first, even though he took a ride on the fox. But Charlie didn't stay to argue. He'd learned to keep his head down when other people got unreasonable, and come back with another idea next time. Wayne knew he would, of course. And Wayne was right.

Chapter Three

Winter really started that week. Most mornings it was so foggy and cold Miss Tinsdale let her littles go straight in without waiting for the whistle. The puddles were frozen over with crackly ice that broke when bikes went through it and Mr Flint lit paraffin lamps in the toilets to stop them freezing up.

Old man Perkins must have been pleased with it all because he sold paraffin and candles round the houses in case of power cuts and all that. Nobody bought any of it while the sun was shining. Winter was the only time of the year when people were actually glad to see him.

He had his cows too, of course, but they didn't do much in the winter. When the spring came, he always took them for walks round the village to fatten them up. His own field round the back of his yard was that patchy with dandelions and nettles, there wasn't very much for a hungry cow to grow big and strong on, so he took them all for walks where they could have a munch for free. They ate the grass off the side of the road, people's flower beds, the Lime Kiln's window boxes, bedding plants for sale outside Pearson's, just about anything they could wrap their tongues round. Sometimes he just shoved them out and let them wander round for a nature ramble on their own, and made Biddy bring them back when she got in from school. It wasn't surprising no one thought much of old man Perkins while the sun was shining.

When Ma Perkins brought the cows in for him, she had her own special way. She never went trotting round the moors looking for them. All she did was open her kitchen window and let go her cow yell. The cows always heard her, even if they were round the other side of the hill.

She used the same sort of yell when she wanted Biddy, only she changed the words.

"Bee-Dee!" Lots of people said they could hear Ma Perkins's yell even when they were right down by the freezer inside Pearson's.

Biddy sometimes got her mum's cow yell mixed up with her Biddy yell, and she trotted off home when she wasn't wanted. It was odd really, because the cows always got it right.

Wherever Biddy went, she skipped. She didn't have a skipping rope or anything, she just skipped along without one, singing to herself for company. It was never hard to tell it was Biddy Perkins, even from miles away! When she met people she skipped off to one side to be out of the way, or she pretended to do her laces up till

they'd gone on. When it was Coppins's lot she kept on skipping, because they played leap-frog over her if she was down with her shoes.

Charlie and his lot just walked round shouting at each other like they were so far apart they really needed radios.

"You really reckon you're going to make money out of it?" Wayne was yelling. They were on their way back to the classroom from buying Mr Greysock's crumpets because he was on dinner duty. "Pedal-powered planes were invented years ago. They've even pedalled them across to France. Your brilliant idea's just as new as if you invented cow pats!"

Colin Dibble came trotting over. Dibble had

his dinner at home with his mum. Wayne yelled a message. "You're just in time to say goodbye to Charlie. He's pedalling off into space. Do you want him to take any messages?"

"You don't believe nothing, you don't," Charlie said. "That pilot who pedalled across to France, he had to go over water didn't he. If he'd flown over houses and people, he'd be risking lives if he got tired and fell out of the sky. My idea's quite different. You stay all bright and fresh because you don't go knocking yourself out just getting off the ground. There's still that prize going for the longest flight, and it's worth a thousand pounds. Just pedalling to France isn't going to win it."

"Aren't you just weird, Coppins?" Nuttley said. "That lot you're talking about had technology, and back-up teams and got lent money by factories and all that. You've bashed up your own plane in your dad's workshop, and you reckon you're going to win a thousand pounds. I'd like to see it!"

"Give me a day to get some more fertilizer bags from Braddon's yard," Charlie answered. "Then you can."

The man still hadn't come to mend the telly, so Mr Greysock had to think up a lesson for himself.

"We're going to think about inventions," he announced, like he'd found something really special to brighten up everybody's lives with. "I want you to think about inventions that you consider have really changed the course of human history. Choose one that you feel is the most important, and then draw it yourself. If there's time we can paint it too. The best ones can come out and talk about their choice." He sounded very bright about it all.

"Can we do really old-fashioned ones?" Moira Flynn called up from the back. "I'm going to do the wheel."

Mr Greysock put on his tired look. "Well, you can if you want, I suppose," he said. "Can't you think of something a bit more exciting?"

Moira Flynn shook her head.

"All right, do a wheel then. Make sure it fills the whole page. What are you going to do, Charlie?"

Mr Greysock always asked the fidgety ones first, just to make sure they got on with something.

Charlie came straight out with his answer. "I'm doing pedal-powered flight," he answered. "My invention's so new it hasn't been invented yet."

Everybody got their heads down. The only sound was Biddy Perkins getting a bit of help from Mr Greysock and Moira Flynn showing off zipping up her fancy pencil case every time she took something out.

Then Nuttley had to spoil it all. He shouted it out just as though Mr Greysock wasn't in the room. "Well, just look at that then," he called out. "Just look at that!"

"You got troubles, Nuttley?" Mr Greysock got up out of his chair like he was coming over to give Nuttley a few more. "Would it help to send them away if I got in nice and close and slapped your ears for a bit? It's been known to work before."

Wayne got back into his chair. "No, Sir. It's all right thank you, Sir. I just saw it out of the window, that's all. Farmer Braddon's trailer's just gone past. It had a great big dead cow on it."

All the sniffy ones had to go "Yerk" and "Yuk", of course.

"Must Wayne be so disgusting?" Mandy Thommas called out.

"We must all have seen a dead animal before, Wayne Nuttley," Mr Greysock said, all airy. "They need to get that way so we kindly humans can eat them."

"But it only had three legs," Wayne said.

"When my uncle died, he had only one," Mr Greysock answered. "Are you suggesting that cows with three legs ought to live for ever? Everybody has to die come the end, you know.

Even cows with five legs."

Wayne sat back like he wasn't sure if something odd wasn't going on. Old Greasy could be dead thick at times.

At the end, Mr Greysock came sliding round to find the best picture. Some of them were really strange. Marlene Toms had done a whole set of disco lights. She explained that she'd chosen them because her life had never been the same since she'd discovered disco lights. Arthur Sills had come up with a giant fan like windmill on the top of a hill. He said it was to blow the clouds away if people didn't want it to rain. Susan Burt's drawing was an aerosol can full of cat smell for scaring off mice without having to flatten their heads. The last one to get chosen was Charlie's.

It wasn't that often that Charlie got his pictures chosen, so people sat up for a look. Wayne Nuttley put on his bored look and leaned back on his chair, but he still watched.

Charlie had drawn a glider. Its wings stretched right across from one corner of the paper to the other, all in the blue felt tip Mr Greysock had let him borrow. What you noticed first were its wheels. They were one behind the other like a bicycle, and it had pedals for the pilot to put his feet on. The back wheel was the oddest bit. It was fitted with bits of cardboard or something like that, to make it look like a giant fan. Perhaps it was a flying hair dryer. Charlie had gone to a lot of trouble.

Tansy Meredith said she'd seen it before, because her dad had a picture of it in his guide book to China, but it didn't bother Charlie. He just stood there in the gangway, holding it above his head like he was selling it at an art gallery.

"We've still got five minutes till the bell," Mr Greysock said. "Bring it up and I'll clip it on the blackboard so you can give us a talk on it."

Charlie shuffled up to the front, wiped his nose, pulled his jeans up as far as he could get them, took a long look at his picture like he'd never seen it before, and started up.

"This is a picture of the plane that's going to win the prize for the longest flight of a pedal-powered aeroplane," he said, all loud and clear. He pointed to the middle bit with the pilot sitting on it. "This is the pedalling unit," he said. "The pilot sits on his pedalling unit and pedals his propellor round like it was his back wheel." He stepped back and had another look. "This is the wing. It clips on his front handlebars when he's going fast enough for take-off." He stepped back again, to make sure he hadn't missed anything. "And that's the ground, down here. That's it really."

Mr Greysock had gone off to sit in Charlie's chair while Charlie was up at the front giving his talk. "Well, tell us what's so special about your pedal-powered plane, Charlie," he called out. "Aren't all pedal-powered planes like that?"

Charlie shook his head. "Mine's special because it comes in two parts," he said. "There's the pedalling unit, here, and there's the wing, that's this part here." He stepped across to his picture and tapped it with the blackboard cleaner like he was an army general telling his soldiers where to go. "My plane comes in two parts because of the rules."

"The rules?" said Mr Greysock. He wasn't giving anyone else much chance to ask questions.

"There's rules for the competition," Charlie said, all patient. "The rules don't let people pull their planes along with cars and things. They're not allowed to roll them down hills so they can get fast enough for take-off. They've got to pedal them along the ground. Most pilots get that tired just pedalling their planes along the runway, they're all beat in by the time they've got up into the air. That's why nobody's gone that far yet."

"Won't yours be the same then?" Mr Greysock seemed very interested. "Won't your plane be just as heavy as the others?"

Charlie shook his head again. "When I pedal

off down the runway, I'll only be half as heavy as anybody else because my plane won't have its wing on," he said. "My works team will have it. They'll be waiting down at the other end of the runway with it, holding it just right so my pedal unit can clunk into it the moment it gets there. I'll be going that fast, all I'll need do is lean back and fly off. With my back wheel propeller, I'll be able to go just as far as I want. That's my invention."

"Well now, isn't that something?" Mr Greysock said to everybody. "That's what I call a real thought-out invention. Do you think it could ever really happen?"

"Oh yes, it could happen," Charlie answered. "It could happen any day now."

"I think we'll put it up over the nature table where we can all see it," Mr Greysock said. "Who knows, one day, Charlie's pedal-powered machine could change all our lives!"

Mr Greysock didn't often get things right, but this time, just for once, he'd come very close to it.

It had been really cold and foggy all day. Farmer Braddon's private yellow fog rolling in over the wall from his muck heap hadn't helped. It go so dark after dinner, Miss Tinsdale's littles were sent home early.

When the chip van came creeping round with only brown blobs instead of headlights, Charlie was the only customer. He stayed in the yellow light from the hatchway to eat his Fatty Scratchings before they got cold, but while he was blowing the ones on the top of his bag so he could get his fingers in, someone out in the fog called his name. He squinted out to see who it was, and in from the dark stepped Biddy Perkins.

"You seen Meatloaf?" Biddy asked.

Charlie kept on munching, watching her over his bag.

"He's gone off," Biddy said. "You seen him?"

Charlie shook his head.

"He's bit through his rope again and gone off."

Something with corners on stuck in Charlie's throat. He had a go at coughing it up.

Biddy hadn't finished her conversation. "Mum

sent me out to see where he's got to. You've not seen him then?"

Charlie wiped the tears out of his eyes. "Why d'you reckon I'd know where that mad thing's gone?" he said. "He's given me enough trouble already without me trotting round looking for more." He went back to digging the last Fatty Scratching out of the bag. When he looked up, Biddy Perkins had gone.

"That's it for tonight," the chip man called. "If I don't get off now, I'll be stuck here for the night. Mind your head." He swung the hatch shut, climbed through to his seat and drove the van off up the lane.

Charlie stood in the dripping dark. Once the van had rumbled off, it went so quiet he felt he'd gone deaf. He tiptoed across the grass to the road, feeling the edge with his foot and holding out his arms to save barging into things.

He had just reached the path up to Railway Cottages when he stopped. He stood quite still, with his head tilted like he was listening.

"Meatloaf?" he whispered. "That you, Meatloaf? Here, boy, over here! It's only me!"

Nothing much happened. He stood there for a little while longer and then turned to walk on up the path. Then he stopped again.

"Meatloaf?" He called out quite sharp this time.

"If that's you being funny out there! Get off home!" He tilted his head again. "Meatloaf?"

Then he suddenly took off and ran, stumbling up the path and flicking his head round to see what was coming. When he got to his back door he was sobbing for breath.

He had to scrabble round under the mat for the key. He was that keen to get it open he missed the keyhole twice. Then he barged the door open and fell inside, kicking it shut from where he lay.

Charlie must have reckoned he'd be all right once he was home. But then he remembered, when he felt along the wall for the light switch. He hadn't any money for the meter.

Chapter Four

Charlie was inside in the warm early next morning while everybody else was still outside, fog-horning their way round in the cold, waiting for Mr Greysock to come out and blow the whistle.

"Special assembly," Mr Greysock shouted, while people came tramping through. "We won't need hymn books. Give me a second to get this down and we'll go on through."

It was remarkable how Mr Greysock got himself comfortable on days when everybody else was trooping around in the cold and the wet. This time, he had his mug full of tea and he'd wandered into the classroom with his coat still on. Anyone else trying that would have got slung straight out and given the wellies to tidy for a week.

The usual people looked anxious on the way in, of course. Special assemblies always meant something odd was happening. Charlie Coppins had his head down. He always had to stand back and be the last in the line going into assembly, because Mr Greysock had made a special place for him on the end of the line. He got called up to the platform that often it saved him treading on people on his way out.

When he came in and saw who had come to assembly, he stepped back out through the hall door again, just like it was an action replay on the telly done backwards. If Mr Greysock hadn't been coming in behind him, Charlie would have walked all the way back to his breakfast. He got shoved along into his place so he could look up at the visitor like everybody else.

Up on the platform, waiting by her bookstand, stood Mrs Trugg. Beside her stood Sergeant Edgely.

Mrs Trugg started up. Nobody ever fidgeted while it was Mrs Trugg. She was that sharp she could even spot people's eyes moving off her while she was talking. Anyone coughing got slung outside. She never missed a thing. She always kept her glasses on for when she had to read from her book, but she took them off for looking at people.

When she really got going she whipped them off so fast it brought her hair down. Sometimes, if lots of people came in for a mention, she finished assembly looking like she'd come into school through the hedge.

"Come along children," she called out sweetly, using the encouraging voice she kept for visitors. "We have a friend come to see us this morning, so let's show him how our manners shine, even on the darkest day."

Just to make sure that her little message had reached certain people not famous for their shiny manners, she drew her glasses delicately off her nose and let them bounce on their string across the front of her cardigan. Then she switched her warm and friendly smile back on again and stepped away from her bookstand. "Would you like to talk to us all now, Sergeant?" she said. "Everybody's ready."

Sergeant Edgely always looked different without his hat on, even though it left a red line across his forehead showing where it had been. He stepped forward to Mrs Trugg's bookstand, put a little cough into his hand and started up.

"I have to report," he announced, "that yesterday afternoon, a cow owned by Farmer Braddon was brutally savaged to death by some other animal as yet unknown."

He might have started off a bit better. The

littles right below him still weren't sure why he was taking assembly, and one of the really tiddly little ones on the end started to sob like it was her very own cow he was talking about. Miss Tinsdale leaped over and carried her out.

While all that was going on, most of Mr Greysock's lot were turning round for a stare and a nudge at Wayne Nuttley. All Wayne could do was scowl back like he had no idea why he was suddenly so interesting. Sergeant Edgely tried again.

"What I meant to say, children, is that yesterday afternoon, one of Farmer Braddon's cows got herself hurt quite a lot, and she couldn't get herself better again and we don't know how it happened. Well, we do know how it happened, but we don't know who did it." He looked anxiously round at Mrs Trugg to see if his new way of saying things was any better. "I just want to know if any of you children might have seen a strange animal hanging round the village yesterday. Yes, young man?"

Wayne Nuttley's hand was up. Everybody twitched round for a stare, of course. Mrs Trugg got up to see who it was.

"I saw it," Wayne called up. "It was on the back of Farmer Braddon's trailer. One of its legs had come off. I told Mr Greysock. It was dead by then though."

"Ah," Sergeant Edgely said. "Yes, that was very observant of you. What I really want to know, though, is how it happened. Has anyone seen a stray dog or anything like that lurking round? One they haven't seen before?"

Everybody set up a buzz. How hungry did a stray dog need to be to want a cow's leg for its tea? The littles down the front were all shaking their heads like they were making sure nobody thought it was them.

"Yes, that young man at the side there."

Everybody jumped. It was Charlie Coppins.

"I was out in the fog last night," Charlie called up.

"And you saw a stray dog?"

"No. I didn't see no strange dog. I just met someone out looking for theirs, that's all. He'd bitten through his rope and run off."

"Do you know whose dog it was?"

"Yes."

Mrs Trugg had got up again so she could join in. "Come along then, Charlie Coppins," she called down. "Sergeant Edgely only wants to help. Speak up, boy."

"It was Biddy Perkins's Meatloaf."

Mrs Trugg opened her mouth to say something back, but somebody else beat her to it. Another voice came splitting up from the middle of the hall.

"He bleedin' never! Meatloaf come on straight home. Anyone says Meatloaf's killed anything is a bleedin' liar!"

It was Biddy Perkins! Biddy Perkins who never said a word to anyone. She was so quiet that lots of people didn't even know what her voice was like, and here she was swearing round the place like her bolts had worked loose.

It worked wonders on Mrs Trugg. She set off skipping along the front of the platform with her glasses dancing about on their string, trying to find a quick way down because Sergeant Edgely was in the way of the steps. Some more of Miss Tinsdale's littles set up crying because of all the shouting, and Mr Flint came trotting in with his bucket because he thought someone had been sick.

The only one not jumping around and having a say was Biddy Perkins. Anyone else, and Mr Greysock would have gone in and slapped their ears off, but all he did was put his arm round Biddy's shoulders. It was more like it was Biddy who'd been upset, and everybody else was to blame. There she stood, with her head under his jacket and sucking her thumb, staring out at the world through her foggy glasses, like a chick got in under its mother.

When he said it was special assembly, Mr

Greysock couldn't have reckoned it was going to be that special.

At going home time, Charlie slipped off home without waiting to see if the chip van had made it through the fog. Wayne Nuttley did his deliveries, but he had to push his bike round, the fog was that thick. He was just putting his last box on his basket when who should come skipping up the passage but Charlie, puffing for breath like he'd run all the way back down from his house with his own private radar.

"I thought you'd gone on home for your tea," Wayne said. "You haven't been waiting for the chip van all this time have you?"

Charlie shook his head. "I've been home and out again," he said. "It's finished. All ready to see. You coming up?"

"I'm going on home for tea," Wayne said. "What's finished, anyway?"

"The plane," Charlie answered. "The plane. I got some more fertilizer bags off old Braddon on the way home. The wing's finished. That makes all of it."

"It better be worth the trouble," Wayne said. "We'll get Dibble on the way. I've got to drop this box off for his mum."

They stumbled off through the fog. Colin

wasn't that keen on coming out, seeing he was indoors for the night and the fog would bring his cough back, but Charlie told him Marlene Toms would get his place on the works team if he missed the unveiling ceremony, and he'd just have to watch with the spectators.

It's odd how difficult it is for three people to walk along a path when the one at the back wants to make sure he doesn't get left behind. Dibble kept in so close, waving his torch around in the fog like some kind of wild disco light, that Wayne made Charlie change places so he could have a turn at getting trodden on.

When they got to Railway Cottages, Charlie took them round the back of the next door house, hauled back some shuttering over the back door and switched on a light. It was his dad's workshop.

There were wooden crates and cardboard boxes, road signs, car tyres, bee hives, oil drums and all sorts stacked up the walls. The window was covered over with a painted sign saying "Get your Xmas Special Here" with a picture of a rocking horse underneath. In the middle of the floor stood a long lumpy shape, covered over by an oily car rug. Charlie stepped over to the rug, took hold, and twitched it off. It was his bike. Upside down on its saddle.

Wayne whistled. "Wow," he said respectfully.

"I am impressed. It's your bike, upside down on its saddle. Look, Colin. Charlie brought us all this way to show us his bike upside down. That's really something."

"It's not just my bike," Charlie answered. "Take a proper look. What's different about it?"

Wayne walked round it. Charlie's bike was different from anyone else's anyway. His dad had done it up as a designer special just for Charlie. It was bright red with the paint the telephone man left in the phone box while they were off having their dinner, and it had the widest handlebars of all the bikes in the world. When the builders had moved the Lime Kiln toilets indoors, they'd slung the old pipes out into the car-park, so Charlie's Dad had taken them for handlebars. They were so wide, if Charlie wanted to hold on to the ends, he had to reach out as far as his arms could stretch. When he was stretched out that far, he looked like he was lying down, with his nose flat on his front lamp. It made it difficult seeing where he was going, of course, because he had to pull his head right back just to see straight ahead. If he put it down again, he ran the risk of knocking himself out with his knees. Charlie's bike was special all right.

Wayne came round to the front. "Your back wheel's gone funny," he said. "That's not how your dad left it."

He was right. Charlie's back wheel wasn't anything like his dad had left it. There were long strips of tin fitted into the spokes. They looked like flattened bean tins out of his mum's dustbin, lined up inside the wheel so it all looked like a giant electric fan.

Charlie watched Wayne, while Wayne watched the wheel. "That's my propeller," he said. "Once I'm actually flying, that'll keep me up there just as long as I want."

"You'll have to wrap up snug," Colin said. "I bet you won't stay up long. It'll be too cold. Planes get ice all over them when they get that cold."

"Watch this then," Charlie said. He leaned over and took hold of one the pedals. "Just feel the air it shifts," he called. "There's real power here!"

His wheel began to move. Then it got up speed till it was whizzing round so fast the fan blades had all joined up into a grey blur, flinging up dust and all sorts. Colin yelled at him to leave off because the dust was getting up his nose, but Charlie didn't notice. "Feel that for power," he was yelling. "Just feel it move!"

Wayne found it difficult getting heard. "Great, Charlie," he shouted over. "Yeah, that's all right, that, Charlie. Charlie, leave it off, will you!"

Charlie straightened up. "Didn't I say?" he panted, all out of breath from flying round the world. "All ready for lift off, you reckon?"

"Lift off?" Wayne answered. "All it's done is lift the dust. If you hadn't been holding that power unit thing up it would have fallen over. Lift off!" Wayne didn't sound that impressed.

"Yeah, but I didn't have forward thrust as well, did I," Charlie said. "It's only to keep me up there while I'm travelling forward as well. By the time I need to use my propeller, I'll have had my big push up into the air. It's only an engine on its test bed, you know. Nobody flies just an engine."

"He'll be pedalling along the ground first," Colin said. "That's what they all have to do. He won't take off till he's going fast enough, like they did on that telly programme. That's what you said, wasn't it, Charlie?"

"Sort of," Charlie answered. "But don't forget my design's different from all that lot. For one thing, my wing won't be fixed to my power unit while I'm getting up speed to fly, so they can't call it a proper plane, it'll just be a power unit getting up speed. There's no rules about power units getting help, just planes. My power unit here only turns into a plane right down at the far end of the runway when it clunks into its wing, and it'll be going so fast by then it'll be ready to fly straight off. It won't be breaking any rules."

"So if you're not going to pedal this rattling great thing down the runway, just how are you

56

planning to get up enough speed to fly then?" Wayne asked. "You planning Farmer Braddon's going to pull you along behind his tractor?"

"No," said Charlie, like he'd got it all worked out, "I'm not using tractors. I'm using gravity."

"Gravity?" Wayne let go a great snort. "It's gravity's going to keep you on the ground. Or are you planning to switch it off?"

Charlie went on like he hadn't heard. "I'll be starting my run down to my wing from the top of the hill," he said. "You watch. By the time I get down to the bottom, my power unit will be travelling quite fast enough. If you lot hold my wing right, I'll just clunk in, lean back and fly off. I reckon it'll be the longest pedal-powered flight ever!"

Wayne didn't answer straight off. He took another walk round Charlie's upside-down power unit. Charlie had really given him something to think about.

"You sure your wing will really clip on the front?" he asked finally. "It won't fall off?"

Charlie shook his head.

"Well you've still missed something out. I knew you would." Wayne sounded pleased. "You've no way of turning corners. All you're going to do is fly in one boring straight line. You're going to have to walk back."

Chapter Five

By Saturday, of course, everybody had forgotten all about Charlie and his world record pedal-powered plane. It was only when Marlene Toms saw Wayne Nuttley and Colin Dibble plodding past Pearson's on either end of an odd looking stretcher all covered with old fertilizer bags, that the word got round.

There was no sign of Charlie Coppins. In dignified silence, Wayne and Colin propped their frame up against the Lime Kiln railings and climbed through to the grass on the other side. Then they dragged their load over the top, carted it over the grass to the bottom of the slope, lowered it carefully to their feet, and waited.

Once Marlene Toms had worked out just what was happening, it didn't take long before most of her lot were out there scrambling up on the railings for the best seats.

Wayne and Colin didn't take any notice of the spectators. They just stood quietly by their section of Charlie's record breaker, like the flight programme was already in operation and the next stage was just about to commence.

The crowd got bigger. Most of Mrs Trugg's lot

were perched up on the top rail like starlings on a phone wire. All the rest had settled on the grass. It was quite odd, really, all those people out in the sunshine when Saturday telly had already started.

"That Charlie's stretcher you've got there then?" Andy Timms called over. "All ready to collect up his bits and cart them off to the graveyard, are we?"

Wayne just shaded his eyes and peered up the hill, taking no notice. It made everyone on the railings turn and stare in the same direction, as though Charlie's plane was already on its way. But then Moira Flynn pointed out that what was lying down there on the grass was Charlie's wing, and until he came down on his pedal unit for his supersonic docking procedure, there was no point in anyone staring anywhere.

After that, the crowd settled down to wait. It must have been quite different for most of them, spending Saturday morning squashed up on a railing, waiting for Farmer Braddon's collection of old fertilizer bags to leap off the ground and flap away over the church roof.

Then Charlie appeared. Marlene Toms let go a squeal because he came in from behind them all, across the car park, and she hadn't been expecting him.

He came trudging across the gravel with his head down and his bicycle hooked up on his shoulder, like he was deep in private thought. The top rail spectators gave him a jeering cheer. Some of the others even clapped.

He must have come all the way down from Railway Cottages with his bike up on his shoulder. The moment he put it down on the ground and Wayne helped get it over the railings it became clear why he hadn't been riding it. He'd done something different to his back wheel.

"Like the paddle wheel," Daryl Manners shouted over. "You're going the wrong way with your paddle boat. The stream's over there!"

"That's not a paddle wheel." Andy Timms had to have his say as well, of course. "It's Charlie's electric fan in case he gets too close to the sun and he wants to cool down. Watch out your tyres don't pop, Charlie!"

Charlie didn't shout anything back. He just shouldered his bike and faced up the slope while Wayne went back to the wing.

It was a long haul up the hill any time, let alone for someone with a bike wrapped round his neck. Halfway up, Charlie put his load down on the grass and turned to stare back at his helpers as though he was measuring how far he'd climbed. More likely, he was just getting his breath back so his legs would stop wobbling.

Nuttley and Dibble were too busy doing all sorts to stare back. They'd picked up the wing so that the two slots where Charlie's handle bars were going to fit were facing up the hill. Then they practised holding it with their finger tips, so that when Charlie's pedal unit docked, their fingers wouldn't get taken away as well. They seemed to know exactly what to do.

It was nearly time. There he stood on the top of the hill, sharp and dark on the skyline with the sun showing up the gaps where his jeans didn't reach. Even that far off, there was no mistaking it was Charlie.

His voice came floating down to the watching crowd. He had turned his bike to face down the runway. "Left a bit!"

The works team shunted over.

"Back a bit!"

The works team shunted back.

"Check your heights."

Wayne suddenly reached down and pulled a stick out of his welly nobody had noticed before. Colin Dibble did the same. Wayne stood his stick on the ground and carefully rested his end of the wing on the top. Dibble fiddled about, dropped his stick twice, got it right, and settled down on his knees, holding his end of the wing to keep it at the right height for Charlie's handlebars.

Most people could have worked out what was going on without Moira Flynn giving a running commentary, but she reckoned she was doing everybody a favour by droning on like she'd seen it done a hundred times before.

One thing, though, was clear to everybody. If Charlie didn't come down fast enough, then he wouldn't take off fast enough, and if that happened, then he'd come down on the most unfortunate place he could hope to choose, the church roof. The last time Mr Bastable caught Charlie up there, he'd promised he'd hang Charlie up with the bells if he caught him again, and ring him twice a day till Christmas.

It went very quiet.

"Ready?" It was Charlie's last word.

"Ready for countdown." It was Wayne Nuttley who yelled back. Dibble was down on his knees

with his eyes shut.

At that moment, the church clock set up bonging ten o'clock. Charlie swung his leg over the saddle. It didn't seem too clear whether he was waiting for the bell to stop before he started his countdown, or he was using it up there for a countdown of his own.

Andy Timms and his lot weren't sure either, so they set up chanting in time with Mr Bastable's bell.

"Five! Four! Three! Two! One! Lift-Off!!"

Silence.

Charlie's feet were up on his pedals, but it wasn't easy to see if he was moving. Then, suddenly, he wasn't on the skyline any more. His mission had begun.

At first, his speed didn't seem that impressive, but once he started kangarooing over the heaps

63

and the mole hills, all rock hard and solid in the cold, he looked like he was picking up all the speed he wanted.

He was lying low to reduce wind resistance, with his hands out at the far end of his handlebars and his head down over his front wheel. He was standing up on his pedals so his legs could take the shock, but that had left space for the saddle to come smacking up from underneath every time he hit a bump. It all looked very uncomfortable.

Charlie's head looked like it was going to flick off. Everybody was so interested in watching what was happening up at the front of the travelling pedal unit, that nobody noticed what was happening at the back. Not till Wayne yelled.

At first it looked like lumps of mud flying up behind Charlie's back wheel, just like the way horses kick up lumps of mud when they come through with the hunt. Wayne knew it wasn't lumps of the hill flying about though.

"Look out for your propeller, Charlie," he yelled. "Your propeller! It's working loose!"

What happened next must have surprised some of the crowd. Even though Moira Flynn had been telling them all, there must have been quite a few dimmos who had no real idea about Charlie's flight plan. Colin Dibble missed most of it because he was down on the grass with his eyes shut. It surprised Wayne Nuttley though. He just stood there staring, like it was all more than he'd reckoned on, even though he'd been in on it from the start. It must have surprised even Charlie.

He flew all right. On that day, and at that time, Charlie Coppins really flew. Even after Marlene Toms left off screaming and let go of Andrea Dimmock, she never said he hadn't, and she was never one to let Coppins get away with a thing. People had all sorts of different ideas, of course. Once they got to talking to Dibble afterwards they all said what they'd been expecting. Nuttley wasn't there, because he'd gone off to Castlebury.

For someone attempting a world record, Charlie must have had a lot to think about. He had that long ride down to the bottom of the hill, with lumps and bumps on the way to manage. He had to make a spot-on docking procedure with his wing, and he had to get up enough speed for a perfect take-off. It couldn't have been easy. What with his head getting flicked about by his handle-bars, and his bottom getting smacked about by his saddle, it was no wonder Charlie's last problem took him by surprise.

He'd started his run quite slowly, but when he hit that last ant heap, he was truly supersonic.

That was when he flew. In a graceful curve, Charlie took his pedal unit, handlebars, paddle wheel and himself, up and away into the sunny sky, far above his work's team's heads, far above his waiting wing, and over the Lime Kiln railings into the car-park beyond.

Everybody heard his breath leave him when he hit the ground. He came down with such a smack, showering up the gravel stones and flopping along the cobbles in such a tangle of arms and legs and bike bits, that the first people who got to him gave up trying to help, and waited for the ambulance men to do it instead.

The ambulance came so quickly, it was just like it had been waiting round the corner for Charlie to land. It came crunching in over the gravel without even blowing its dee-dah. The driver was leaning out of his window.

66

"Bit of trouble then?" he called.

"Lad's come off his bike," one of the grown-ups who'd come running out of the Lime Kiln called over. It was odd really. The people who got to Charlie first didn't belong in Long Tussocks. They were just driving through on a holiday. "You'd better be quick. Someone ought to get his parents."

That struck everybody silent, of course. Charlie Coppins was just about to fly away from this world, when only moments ago they'd been cheering him on his way. Another ambulance man jumped down and ran round to open the back doors. Then he slid out a stretcher so he could gather in the body. At that moment though, Charlie sat up. He wasn't dead, the ambulance man explained. He just deserved to be. They would take him in all the same, just to make sure.

Everybody changed straight off, of course. A poor, dead Charlie was worth a few sobs, but a wicked, live Charlie needed a good smack round the ear for frightening people like that.

Oddly enough, someone was already in the ambulance, wrapped up in a red blanket on the other stretcher. "Quietly does it then," said the ambulance man, and clicked shut the door.

The engine started. "Someone better tell his mum," said the ambulance man out of his window. "I can't hang about. Got to get this other one in." And off it went.

Wayne Nuttley followed on his bike, all the way into Castlebury hospital, but when they took Charlie inside he didn't know who to ask, so he came on home again.

It was quite a different Saturday from the usual ones, that Saturday Charlie went for the world pedal-powered flight record. For one thing, Charlie had been taken off to hospital, and for another, the fog had blown away. Nobody found out who the other person in the ambulance had been till Mrs Pearson found Biddy Perkins sniffling round the freezer buying her mum some supper. Biddy's dad had been the other one.

He'd fallen through their chicken house roof trying to find where their chickens hid their eggs. Mrs Pearson spread the news round quick enough, of course, but nobody was that upset. If Mr Perkins bought his eggs from Pearson's Stores like everybody else, he wouldn't have ended up where he was.

Charlie stayed in hospital all night, just so they could make sure he wasn't hurt anywhere else. His mum brought him home in a taxi next morning, but nobody turned out to see him because it was their Sunday lie-in. The fog had come back anyway. Perhaps it would have been better for Charlie if it had never gone away.

Chapter Six

Everybody came in on Monday morning expecting Mrs Trugg to drag Charlie up on the platform, but as it was he hardly got a mention.

He was keeping his head down, of course. He stayed in the caretaker's hole till the whistle went, and then he slid back into the classroom making sure no one noticed his leg had gone stiff with the sticky plaster. He had a tear in his jeans where the sticky plaster showed through, but that was all that was different.

When it came to assembly Mr Greysock said Charlie could stay in the classroom if he wanted and give out the test papers for when everybody came back in. It might have made Charlie a bit nervous seeing Mr Greysock acting so kind and thoughtful, but he never said.

Once the hymn was over Mrs Trugg went on about people who tried to kill themselves, frightening sensible children who should have stayed indoors watching their tellies, but that was all. Biddy's dad got a mention because he shouldn't have fallen off his ladder. People should be kind to those who fell off ladders, but they didn't need to be kind to stupid boys who fell off bicycles.

It was hard to work out what Biddy Perkins was thinking, with her dad being talked about in assembly. Some of the girls turned round and gave her brave smiles, but it wasn't easy to see her eyes through her foggy glasses to work out if she was smiling back.

It hadn't surprised anybody really, hearing about Mr Perkins falling off his ladder. He fell off a lot of things. They didn't let him back in the Lime Kiln the last time he fell over. He'd gone down after he smacked Ken Widgery round the ear, and Mr Sansom had thrown them both out for knocking his furniture about. After that, Mr Perkins took to going off up the lane to some other pub for his scrumpy, taking his bike along with him like he always did, so it could hold him up while he walked back.

Mrs Trugg brightened up once she'd finished with the accident victims. "Now children," she announced, "we have something really important to talk about, something very, very special."

She always started up like that when something really boring was coming. She made it sound like she had secret news that the school was closing down and everybody was going to get paid to stay at home.

"Not one of us, I'm sure, has forgotten that dreadful day last week when Sergeant Edgely came in to talk to us about Farmer Braddon's cow, so badly treated by that wild dog still wandering about – " and she stopped to gaze out through the window over the piano " – out there."

Of course everybody turned to stare out through the window as well, just as though they were expecting something wild and dripping with dribble to have its black nose pressed tight up against the glass.

Mrs Trugg turned back to look at everybody. She slowly lowered her glasses off her nose, and then peered right down to the end of the hall to make sure even Mr Greysock got the news.

"IT HAS HAPPENED AGAIN!"

That really worked. The ones who hadn't jumped clean off the floor all on their own grabbed their next door neighbour instead. Even Mr Greysock came straight up off the wall by the light switch. Everyone went deadly quiet, ready for the next terrible news flash. Everyone, that is, except for Wayne Nuttley. He shot up his hand, and he was wriggling about like he was too late for the toilet.

"Please, Miss," he called out from his line. "I've seen it. Up Tussocks Lane. Sergeant Edgely was there. It's a sheep. But there's another one, up the back of the trough in Mr Tullet's paddock. It's got all its tubes hanging out. There was only half of its bits left when I – "

"Thank you, Wayne Nuttley," Mrs Trugg

called down. "You can leave out all that coarse information none of us has asked for. If there's a record for people getting to the scene of a tragedy before anybody else, it must surely go to you." And she put her glasses back on her nose.

Wayne muttered something dark and horrible into the floor and Mr Greysock leaned in and gave him a push.

"Now then, children," Mrs Trugg said, "while all this is going on, every one of you is to go straight home once the end of the day bell goes. No dawdling on the way. School gate to your gate. Is that understood? Only very, very stupid people dawdle about in the fog, placing temptation in the way of hungry animals."

Everybody nodded. They were real nods too. Any dimmo who wanted to hang around in the cold so he could get his bits pulled out deserved all he got.

On wet playtimes, Mr Greysock always shoved everybody out to the toilet whether they felt like going or not. It meant nobody had the chance to ask once lessons began again. Outside was so cold and foggy that morning, people only got as far as the scraper on the outside step, and then they turned round and skipped back in like they'd really been. Coppins and Nuttley slid out with the rest, but they stayed out. Mr Greysock was busy fiddling around with the telly, so he never noticed. They slipped off round to the side by the kitchen wall so they could keep warm by the cooker fan. Most people kept away from the cooker fan hole because it made them smell of chips, but Charlie got tight in close and pulled his shirt out over it so the hot air could blow up inside.

"Why don't they just go on up to old man Perkins and put a nice new bullet right through that bloodthirsty great hound of his?" Nuttley was saying. "It's stupid saying they've got to wait till they actually see him doing it. We all know it's him."

"No, we don't know, not if we haven't seen him," Charlie answered. He'd shoved his head down into his woolly, so he could get the full benefit from the fan hole dinner-smoke. "Meat-loaf's tied up most of the time. I've seen him. Everybody's got it in for old man Perkins. D'you know, when I was in that ambulance, he kept asking me if I was all right, and there he was with one of his legs broken? He fell asleep twice and they had to blow air into him to wake him up, and he said he was sorry he was being a bother. Most people would have been rolling about yelling their heads off. I reckon everybody's got it wrong about him." He pulled his head out, back into the cold. "That's what I reckon," he said.

"Well, nobody else thinks that," Wayne said.

"They all reckon it'll all be over once Meatloaf's out of the way. At least it would stop everybody going round all twitchy, like they were going to get eaten themselves any minute."

"Well, everybody's all got it wrong, haven't they," Charlie said, all sharp. "It's dead easy blaming someone when you don't like him, specially when he's not here. I bet they wouldn't go round saying it out loud if he was still walking round instead of being stuck in bed with his leg tied up. Once people aren't here any more, everybody else reckons they can say what they like."

Wayne looked over to Charlie, but Charlie wasn't saying anything else. He just stood there, his face still dark and puffy where he'd banged it, letting the chip smoke blow up his woolly. Someone started calling from the playground door.

"Telly's started, you lot. Mr Greysock's asking where you've got to." It was Moira Flynn.

Wayne turned to go in, but Charlie hadn't moved.

"You planning to spend the rest of your life on that chip-smoke life-support system?" he called over. "Charlie?"

Charlie shook his head and tucked his shirt in. "I'll be along," he said quietly. "You go on in."

Wayne waited. "You sure you're all right, Charlie?" he asked. It wasn't like Wayne to ask so kindly, twice. "Mum said you should have

stopped home after that bang you got. You could've told old Greasy it gave you such a knock on the head it sent you funny." He looked carefully at Charlie. "You sure it hasn't?"

"Curtains, please, monitors," Mr Greysock called, and he switched the telly off. "Now then, we're going to talk about that programme first, just to make sure we've all understood it, and then I'm going to show you my map of the sky at night. There's one thing we've all learnt from watching that trapper out there in the Arctic wilderness. There are lots of ways of finding our way when there are no sign posts, but what did that hunter use out there in the snowy wastes?"

"He used traps and things!" Charlie Coppins got it out before anyone.

"No, I mean how did he find his way around? What did he use to find out the right way to go? He didn't have a map did he. Mary?"

"He followed the night sky." Trust Mary Scriven. Chances were she'd come trotting in to school next day with a book on it.

Mr Greysock took a deep breath and began again. "Well we're getting a little closer, but he couldn't just follow the sky could he, Mary. It's what he found up there in the sky that was useful to him. Now, what do you think he saw up there in the night sky that helped him make a proper course back to civilization? Wayne, come on."

"Stars?" Wayne said, like he was asking a question back in case he wasn't right.

"That's it, he was studying the stars. Well done." Mr Greysock sounded pleased he'd found someone so sharp. "That's what the programme was all about. He was studying stars. Now, everybody. Here's a hard one, just to sort out the ones who were really watching. Are you ready?" He stopped to let everyone get ready to be the first one back with the answer. "Here it is. So, that trapper we've been watching was studying the stars. Now, why?"

It was Charlie Coppins who got it again, long before any one else. "He had to get back to market to flog off all them furs before the polar bears came back and did him for it," he shouted. "He must have made a packet on that lot!"

Mr Greysock looked like he was quietly praying. "No, Charlie," he said, carefully, taking care his voice didn't frighten anyone. "He wasn't just interested in getting a quick bunk off home to flog off his furs. That is not what the last half hour in the dark with our expensive television was all about. Not one tiny, tiny little bit. And unless someone tells me the right answer very soon, I'm going to creep away and have a little cry inside my cupboard."

"He had to follow the stars because his compass had gone all dizzy what with being so close to the North Pole," Colin Dibble chanted back. Then he turned round and smiled at Charlie.

"That's right, Colin. That trapper might have been slogging round the Arctic knocking poor innocent wildlife on the head, but what we were really meant to notice was his way of navigating his way home. Have you got that, Master Coppins? Have we time to let you come out and tell us all about it?"

The dinner bell had gone. Someone leaned over and hissed into the back of Charlie's head. "You'd better say you've got it, Coppins. It's dinner

77

time!"

A great beam of happiness crossed Charlie's face, like some huge new thought had just sunk down through his hair from a high and beautiful place. "Yes, I've got it now," he said gratefully. "I've really got it. Thank you."

Mr Greysock couldn't have been hungry because he wasn't bothering with the bell. "Well, Charlie," he said, all kindly, "tell us all about it then."

Charlie didn't look one bit nervous, even though Andy Timms and Daryl Manners and all that lot were hissing at him from behind. He took a deep breath. "That trapper with the rabbit on his head worked out that if he followed the stars instead of his dizzy compass, he could nip off home twice as quick and flog all his skins off in time for market day. I reckon he must have made a fortune every trip. All them furry little animals, just sitting there waiting for him to come round and slice their skins off. And he got them all for free. He didn't have to feed them till they were big enough to knock on the head like Farmer Braddon does. He just picked them off the ground. That's the way to make money. If I had a job like that I could make enough money in no time. I bet he spends all summer with his dad having a holiday on the beach with a surf board!"

Even after the dinner ladies had stacked all the tables back up again, Charlie was still twittering on about it. "Just think of all those fur coats in the fashion mags," he said. "They sell for thousands. All you've got to do is find some animal and take its skin off and you can make the same."

"You can't go killing things just so rich people can show off they've got money," Wayne said. "You can't do that, even to bog-rats. They've got rights too."

Charlie thought a bit before he came back with an answer. "All right then," he said. "But that doesn't stop you finding animals that have died already. They're not going to be bothered that much if I took their fur off once they'd died."

"And just how many furry animals lie round the place all nice and dead just so you can take their fur off them, bozo?" Wayne asked. "Your fortune's going to take a long time coming if you've got to wait round for that to happen."

Charlie didn't answer straight off, but it was plain he was thinking about it. "Well I bet there's a way," he said finally. "I'm going to work it out somehow. I'll find a way, you'll see. And don't you go thinking you can come on holiday too. Not unless you bring your own surf board."

Chapter Seven

Colin Dibble joined Wayne round at the fan hole when he got in from having his dinner at home. Charlie was still inside finishing up some leftovers because Mrs Trugg had got the dinner numbers wrong.

"Did you notice Coppins in that telly lesson?" Wayne asked, all gloomy. "I reckon they didn't check his head properly when they took him in the hospital. He went on about that fur business all the way through dinner. He never stopped. He reckons there's a fortune waiting for him out there somewhere, selling fur coats and all that, and he's going to spend it all taking his dad off for some stupid holiday in the sun. I bet his dad's never neard of it. His mum says it's dead stupid too, but Charlie keeps on about it like it's real."

"It's not just that," Colin put in. "He was going on about people being unfair to Ma Perkins now her old man's gone and done his leg in. Everybody knows Meatloaf's the killer dog, but Charlie goes on like he's the president of the Meatloaf Preservation Society. Damian Tullet told him we'd all be a lot better off if someone did Meatloaf in, and all Charlie did was jump up and smack

Damian round the ear – and Meatloaf's not even his dog!"

"Perhaps we ought to give Charlie the idea that dog fur is all in fashion. He could make a whole set of car seat covers out of that ugly great thing."

"But didn't you hear? He's been off round the Perkins's doing jobs for them. My mum saw him. She was bringing the papers back and she saw him in their yard splitting logs with old man Perkins's chopper. He was smacking it round like he was ringing bells, and it was Sunday too."

"He's still not right then. He was a bit odd out here at playtime." Wayne shook his head. "I said they should have done his head better."

"My mum said that if he goes mixing with that Perkins lot, he's going to end up just as odd as they are."

Unfortunately, it wasn't just Dibble's mum who thought that. Most people made sure they kept out of Ma Perkins's way. It wasn't that difficult, because most times everybody could see her coming. Wherever she went, she always took her pram with her, even when she went down to Pearson's for their late night shopping. It was one of those old-fashioned ones with great big wheels and a hood on to keep the rain off Biddy when she was little. Ma Perkins used it for all sorts, and wherever she went she stacked it up with sticks and logs out of the hedges for their firewood back

home. She stacked it up so high people were always getting caught on the ends of her fuel collection when she went shoving past.

She was never that good at reading, Ma Perkins. When she went round Pearson's shelves looking for things, she always took them down first so she could look at the pictures telling what was inside. Sometimes she got it wrong, and ended up with all sorts she didn't really want. Mrs Pearson helped her by reading out what she'd bought when she got to the till so everybody else standing round could hear. It was the same with the price tickets, because if she got them wrong too she had to go round putting things back. It was dead embarrassing for everybody else when Ma Perkins came in shopping. They all got down to the end by the freezer until she'd gone on home again.

Nobody at school bothered that much with Biddy either. People let her in on their games, but she never remembered the rules so they gave up asking. Most playtimes Biddy sat on the litter bin and watched them. Mr Greysock gave her jobs in the classroom when he saw her on her own, so it didn't bother most people if they left her out.

Biddy's job was putting the paint trays out on Monday afternoons after dinner so that people could get started straight away when they came in. It was always a quiet time, painting. People got their heads down once Mr Greysock gave out what to do and nobody bothered anyone till the bell went.

Mr Greysock was letting all the people who'd finished their pictures pin them up on the back wall to save them curling up when they dried. Charlie was standing on his chair, pinning up Moses In The Bullrushes by C. Coppins next to the Queen. He wasn't really first. It was his last week's picture he'd only just finished. He'd been sent out to tidy the wellies for knocking his water pot over and he'd had to finish it off before he could start his new one.

Away through the wall, Miss Tinsdale's littles were singing their afternoon prayers. All around, brushes were slopping into water pots and people were quietly muttering to themselves while they got things right. Out in front, Biddy Perkins was whispering her page from Radiant Way Book One into Mr Greysock's ear for her special reading lesson. It was that peaceful in there, any one passing by might have thought the whole class had slipped out for a walk.

Then, quite suddenly, a lot of things happened, all at once. Coppins came crashing down off his chair. He didn't drop straight down on the floor like a dead fly off the ceiling either, he came down all arms and legs and sideways, taking Damian Tullet's water pot with him. Tullet jumped up so quick he caught his elbow in Martha Downs's ear and she let go a squeal so wild it brought Mr Greysock round to the front of his desk with a roar all of his own.

"Nobody move," he yelled, which was a bit late seeing that most of the people in the room were already dancing about trying to save their paintings getting ruined in the rush.

Martha Downs had just given Damian Tullet his smack in the ear back, when another surprise joined in. It was Mrs Trugg. The door banged open and in she came, clapping her hands to get everyone's attention.

"Could you all listen a moment, please," she called. "You can all go back to your drama lesson once I've gone. I hope I haven't interrupted you, Mr Greysock, but I need to catch you all before the bell goes. We are having a visitor."

Mr Greysock was already half way down the gangway. From the look on his face it wasn't too clear if he was on his way to help Charlie up off the floor, or pin Charlie up on the wall. He pulled up short and straightened a desk instead.

"Any moment now," Mrs Trugg said. "You will be ready, won't you?" And she swung out. She hadn't noticed that she'd been standing in Damian Tullet's puddle.

"You all heard," Mr Greysock called out. "Get

back to your paintings. If you think you've finished, then do a bit more. We'll clear up when they've gone. Now then, Coppins, just what was all that about? Don't tell me you've managed to find yet another way of destroying civilization as we know it."

It was only then that anybody took the time to look at Charlie. He'd climbed up off the floor and sat down on Martha's chair, but he hadn't answered Mr Greysock. He'd gone dead white and he was breathing hard through his nose like he was going to be sick.

"Charlie?" Mr Greysock came back down the gangway. "Are you all right?"

Charlie didn't look up. He kept on with his hard breathing, staring at the desk top like it was important or he'd fall over in a heap. Then he answered Mr Greysock. It came out all whispery at first, so he swallowed and began again. "They're outside," he said. "One of them pointed up at the window. They've seen me!"

"Who's outside the window, Charlie? For heaven's sake, what are you on about?"

Charlie swallowed some more and then slid down in his seat like it was safer with his head down. "Spacemen," he whispered.

Mr Greysock let go a great yell at that, much bigger than the last one. He smacked the top of

Martha Downs's desk. "You trying to be funny, Coppins? D'you think I'm stupid?"

Charlie struggled up straight. "No, honest, I saw them. They're really out there, a whole row of them. They're going past the railings, on up the hill. They must have come down in the fog. There were – " And then the door opened.

It was Mrs Trugg again, and she had her visitor with her. It was Sergeant Edgely.

"Hullo, Mr Greysock," Sergeant Edgely called. "I'm so sorry to have to interrupt your lesson like this, but I'm afraid something's come up that won't wait. Could I just have a quick word with our friends here?"

Mr Greysock waved his hands like he was offering his friends up as a free gift to anyone who cared to cart them off. "Have them all," he said.

Sergeant Edgely didn't notice Mr Greysock being all flat and bitter. He just walked over and sat on the corner of Moira Flynn's desk. "Just two things to tell you all," he said. "Bad news first and not-so-good news second. First, another two animals have gone, out along Sherbert's Dyke. Same way as the others. Just as well Farmer Braddon's brought all his cows inside, but sheep are still good money lost. There's no doubt about it now. We have a really savage stray on our hands, quite capable of killing two sheep at a

87

time. It's out there, and it's dangerous. You must all of you, every single one of you, be on the look-out for it. On no account must you try to catch it. Tell a grown-up. And if ever you see it, and if you're out there alone at the time . . ." and he stopped so his words could sink in while he let his eyes roam round the room. Then he started up again. "And if you are alone – you would be very wise to run."

It all went dreadfully quiet.

"Do you all understand?"

Everybody nodded. It was too serious to do anything else.

"Good. And now the second piece of news. It's about the ministry men. You'll be seeing them around for quite a while. They came this afternoon, and they won't be leaving till they've done their job. You'll know who they are, because they'll be wearing protective clothing, helmets and overalls and things, to help them with the work they do. As you all know, there's been a lot of talk recently about badgers. Now badgers are beautiful wild animals, but they carry the disease called tuberculosis, and because they use the same fields as the cows, it's been discovered that they're passing their sickness on to them as well. Nobody wants that, of course, because then the disease passes on to their milk. That is why the ministry men are here. They've come to collect up all the

88

badgers living round here, and they're going to take them away till they get better. All they do is pump pois – er, sleeping mixture down their holes where they live and then, once those beautiful creatures are asleep, carry them off till they get better."

He stopped and gave another stern stare round the room so that even the dimmest dimmos could get what he was on about. "On no account go anywhere near the holes where the ministry men have been working. Badgers' sleeping mixture is very, very dangerous stuff for us human beings. Is that clear? Any questions?"

"Yes, please."

Everybody jumped. It was Wayne Nuttley.

"Won't it send the cows to sleep as well?"

"Don't you worry about the cows, sonny," Sergeant Edgely answered. "Farmer Braddon's keeping them in all through the winter, so they're well out of it. By the time they come tripping out again, it will be the spring. That savage stray out there will have been caught, and all those badgers will be better again. The last thing we want is to allow anything to harm those faithful creatures that bring us our daily milk, do we?" He gave away a big, beaming smile. Everybody smiled back, of course, glad of the change. The only one not smiling was Wayne Nuttley.

"Where do they take the badgers off to then?" he asked.

Sergeant Edgely's beaming smile went cold. "I don't know what happens after the ministry men have done their work, son. That's not my business. I'm just here to tell you to keep right out of it." He sounded quite sharp about it all. Perhaps he found all that talk about lugging poor badgers around a bit upsetting.

Mrs Trugg opened the door for him and he waved goodbye. Nobody moved. So many visitors had been popping in through the door it seemed best to wait in case there were some more. It was something quite different that made them turn round. It was a very odd noise, coming from the back. It was Mr Greysock, laughing.

He was leaning up against the back wall while he snorted great gulping sobs into his jacket front. Then he unrolled a lump of tissue out of his pocket so he could dry his tears.

"Coppins," he whispered, not minding at all keeping everybody waiting while he had his own private fit. "You had me going then. You really had me going. Spacemen!" And off he went again.

Of course, everybody else fell about too. After the scare Charlie had given them, and then Sergeant Edgely coming in with his own set of frighteners, it somehow helped things. Charlie didn't laugh. He just sat there, frowning, like he was surrounded by a pack of idiots.

The bell went. Mr Greysock just let everyone go. It didn't seem the right moment for prayers. Charlie slipped out in the rush, but Wayne caught him up.

"Did you hear all that in there?" Wayne said, and he grabbed Charlie's arm to make sure Charlie heard. "It was all lies. They're not digging badgers up to make them better, there's nowhere big enough where they could keep them all. They're here so they can kill them. That's what they're really here for. And you thought they were spacemen! Pity they weren't really. Spacemen would have better things to do."

"You reckon?"

"You heard what old Edgely was on about. Now they're here, there's no way of stopping them. Dead clever, isn't it, telling us once they've already started."

"Let's go over and see what they're doing then," Charlie said. "I saw them on their way up the hill ages back. Wish I hadn't mentioned it now."

They climbed over the railings and took the path behind the school until it turned up the slope. Then they took the sheep track over to the far side. It was strangely silent. Far off in the fog, something was thudding into the ground, like a spade being smacked into tree roots. It was that digging noise that showed them which way to go, but then something else made them stop.

It was a smell. A strange chemical smell, drifting down in the fog. It had a bitter, sharp edge to it, that made them cough. It was the badgers' sleeping mixture.

Chapter Eight

"It's dead wicked," Wayne kept saying while they stumbled back down off the hill. "They're not taking care of those badgers. They're killing them. No wonder we don't get told. You're coming in for tea, aren't you. Mum knows."

Wayne looked over. Charlie hadn't answered. He had his head down and his shoulders hunched up, like he was thinking.

They got to Wayne's path, but Mrs Nuttley pulled the door open before they got to it. "Where've you two been?" she called. "You've not come straight home. You know what Mrs Trugg said. I was getting really anxious."

"We all had to wait till the ministry men had gone on. Sergeant Edgely came into school and told us to keep well away. What's for tea?"

"It's pilchards. And you're lucky they haven't swum off somewhere else." She looked round the side of the door and sniffed. "Lucky you weren't followed," she said.

Charlie still wasn't saying much, even while they were having their tea. Wayne's mum noticed. "Never mind the badgers, Charlie," she said. "It must be for the best if proper official men have come round. After all, what's a few wild creatures if it stops our milk getting that disease in it. You musn't upset yourself. Nature has a way of getting over things. Have some more toast."

"But it's such a waste. All them badgers down there and no one to get them out."

"Well that's a very kind and sensitive thought," Mrs Nuttley said. "Not that many people would have worried." She got up and looked out behind the curtains. "I wish you didn't have all that way up to your house. Make sure you run."

Charlie borrowed Wayne's torch before he trotted off for home. There was something odd about Charlie that made Wayne shake his head.

"Sensitive and thoughtful? Charlie Coppins? He's up to something, that's what he's up to." Wayne watched Charlie's torchlight waving through the trees. "Either that, or he's gone clean off his steaming little porridge-pot. I'm watching you, Coppins."

He turned to go back in, but then he stopped to look up where the door light shone down the path. It was snowing.

In the morning, once everybody saw the state of things, they couldn't get to school fast enough. There was snow everywhere, piled up in the hedges, flattened on the road. It was even glued

all the way up the side of the church tower. It looked like there was even more to come, it was so dark and misty.

Some people had to spoil it straight off, of course. Mr Flint was skipping about in the playground flinging salt everywhere, so no one would bring it in on his mats, and Mr Greysock was happily telling everyone it was going to be wet playtimes all day.

"You can wet your knickers in the snow as much as you like on your way home," he called out. "But I'm not having you lot sitting round my nice dry classroom like a set of leaky duckponds, and that's final."

He had to let people out at playtime though, just so they could go across to the toilets. Charlie and Wayne and Colin Dibble slipped off round to the kitchen fan hole. They weren't there long before Andy Timms went slithering over to the boys' side, with Dave Cork plonking along behind him. It was the odd way Dave went across that made Charlie look over.

"You taken up funny walking then?" he called.

"No, come and look," Dave called back. "I'm making special footprints."

"What's so special about footprints?" Wayne shouted, but they still went over for a look.

"Dad got me new shoes, Saturday," Dave said. "They've got special bottoms on them so they print wild animal footprints when I tread in things. Look." And he printed his boot on a patch of snow Mr Flint's salt had missed. Sure enough, a whole set of paw marks appeared when he took his foot back up.

"That one on this side's a cat," Dave said, pointing. "That one at the top is a fox. Down there's a dog. And this one is a badger. All right, aren't they?"

Charlie got down for a closer look. "They look like real ones," he said, like he was really impressed. "They really do."

"You couldn't make people think a badger had just gone through," Wayne put in. "Not unless he only had one foot. They'd think it was an outing for one footed dogs and cats and foxes as well."

"It's not for that, Nut-case," Dave said. "It's

just so I can tell what animal's gone past. All I have to do is print my foot next door to it, and I can see straight off."

Mary Scriven came picking across from the playground door. She'd even put her wellies on, just to get across to the toilets. "Mr Greysock said you've got to come back in, right now," she said, all sniffy. "Nobody else is allowed out till you're in. He said so."

It was worthwhile getting back in, because Mr Greysock was working out the new lists for handwork. There was all sorts happening. Moira Flynn and her lot hadn't finished their go-cart so they were keeping on with woodwork. A whole crowd were doing printing. Wayne wanted to do bike repairs and Martha Downs had brought her Gramfy's sitting room clock in to mend.

"Well," Mr Greysock said, looking down his list, "that looks like just about everybody. Charlie Coppins, I haven't got anything from you yet. Isn't there some wonder of the modern world you'd like to make?"

"Charlie could make a right mess of anything if you asked him, Sir," Kevin Dobbs called over. He turned round to see if the others were laughing as well.

Charlie didn't laugh. He reached inside his desk and came out with a book. "I want to do sewing," he said.

Just about everybody fell about at that one. Even Mr Greysock had to smile.

"You can all have your little laugh if you want," Charlie said, like he wasn't connected with all the grinning idiots all round him. "I'm going to sew leather things, like they do at the Castlebury leather factory. They make all sorts out there. Nothing wrong in that, is there?"

"There's nothing wrong with it at all, Charlie," Mr Greysock said. "It's a pity some of you others couldn't have thought of something a bit more original. Show me your book then."

It was generally the creepy ones like Moira Flynn and Damian Tullett who brought books and things in to school, but here was Coppins doing it. Colin Dibble turned round to see what Wayne thought about it all, but Wayne was leaning back in his chair looking bored. No one got the chance to say anything more, because Mrs Trugg put her head round the door.

"Just a quick word, Mr Greysock?" she said.

When Mr Greysock came back he went straight over to Biddy Perkins. Biddy was down on the floor in the reading corner sifting through the comic pile. Mr Greysock got down beside her and put his arm round her shoulders. "Your mum's been out looking for Meatloaf," he said. "She's worried he might upset people if he wanders off too far. Sergeant Edgely says they've found his chain undone, so he hasn't broken loose or anything. Have you seen him today?"

It went quiet, while everyone leaned in for a listen. It was hard to see how Biddy was feeling, what with her foggy glasses, but she answered quick enough.

"Meatloaf was all right last night," she said. "Charlie come round to help put him to bed because me dad's off in hospital. Meatloaf was all right then. Charlie fixed his chain. Meatloaf must have undone it for himself."

Mr Greysock got up. "Good girl, Biddy," he said. "I'll pop out and tell them. Don't you worry about Meatloaf. They just want to make sure he doesn't get into trouble." All the same, he was frowning when he opened the door. "That's all they'd better be doing," he said.

"That mad dog of yours, he's gone off for his dinner break, that's what he's done," Andy Timms whispered across while Mr Greysock was out in the corridor. "Lamb chops today then?"

Farmer Braddon's pick-up was outside in the lane. Charlie watched from the window. As Sergeant Edgely walked back across the playground, Farmer Braddon climbed out to get the news. Something slid out of the door while he shut it, and he shoved it back in. Anyone could see what it was. It was his shotgun

Everybody had been nudging and whispering during lessons, but no one came out with anything while Mr Greysock was around. It wasn't till playtime that Andy Timms and his lot started up. "Get Meatloaf!" they set up chanting, once they were out through the playground door and they had Perkins for themselves. Biddy must have set her mind on sliding out before anyone else got going, but one of her wellies didn't turn up till everybody else had theirs on. Charlie was inside helping with the chairs, but he saw it all from the window.

"Get Meatloaf! Get Meatloaf!" They went right up close to Biddy and shouted it through her anorak hood. "They're going to shoot that smelly old hound of yours, Perkins. Can we come and sing at the funeral?"

But right then, all sorts happened. Andy Timms went flapping over backwards like he was doing a gymnastic flip-over. Daryl Manners looked to see why his friend had gone off in so strange a way, but he never got time to see because someone close beside him gave him a smack in the ear. He was a thick and heavy person, Daryl Manners, so a smack in the ear didn't do much except make him curious about where it came from.

"You just just shut your mouth, Timms," Charlie Coppins was yelling. "You just shut your mouth. Get off home, Bid, I'm going to smack your batty mouth flat shut, Timms!"

Timms was backing off, since Charlie was yelling everything just at him, but Daryl Manners wasn't. He had his duffle bag in one hand, and he came back in, swinging it round and round like he was chopping trees. "You trying to muck us about, Coppins?" he yelled, holding his ear with his free hand in case Charlie got through. "You want to muck us about, Coppins?" Manners had his boots in the duffle bag. It must have been just about ready to catch fire it was travelling so fast when it caught Charlie. It stopped him shouting, of course. It sent him off on a little walk of his own, round and round in circles till he dropped to his knees, holding his head all the while to stop the smoke coming out.

A far off window banged open. "You boys! You boys out there shouting! Get Off Home! At Once!" Mrs Trugg's voice came slicing through the fog. "At Once! Did You Hear?"

Charlie didn't look round. He heard the staff-room window slam shut again and Timms and Manners running off, but all he wanted to do was put the fire out. He carefully reached down and

101

scooped a handful of snow off the ground so he could cool his ear.

Voices were still floating over from the other side of the green. "Charlie's gone soft on Perkins, ya-ra, ya-ra. Dirty, dotty Coppins!"

Wayne Nuttley must have finished his tea a long time when the doorbell rang. He was back down on the floor watching the telly, so he took his time getting up to answer it. To his surprise, it was Charlie.

"You said you'd give a hand," Charlie whispered. "I can't get it up the path by the bridge. The snow's too deep up there. I've had to bring it back down again."

Wayne stepped back to let Charlie come in off the step. "You all right?" he asked. "Dibble's just been round saying you had a go at that lot from Moor Lane."

"Yeah," Charlie answered. "Didn't do much good. I'll get them next time, though. Could you come out and give us a pull?"

"What do you want pulled then?" Wayne peered out down the path. "That's a pram out there!"

Charlie nodded. "It's not mine. It's Ma Perkins's. She said I could. I'm using it for my fur trapping." Charlie stopped and thought again. "I haven't told her what I'm using it for."

"What're you lugging bales of straw round at this time of night for? You're not starting up a delivery service for hungry bog rats are you?" Wayne sounded like he was having trouble taking it all in.

"Oh no," Charlie said. "That straw bale's just the cover. I shoved it on top to stop people getting a squint at the cargo."

"So what are you doing then?" Wayne hissed. "I wish you'd get on with it."

"I told you," Charlie said. "It's for my fur trapping. I've got a badger."

"You've got a badger? You've been out in the snow and you've got a badger?" Wayne said it all slow like he didn't want to get it wrong. "You've got a badger in that pram out there?"

Charlie nodded.

"Does it mind?"

"It's dead. You ever seen a live badger sitting up in a pram?"

It was Wayne's turn to nod. "I'll get my wellies," he said. "I'll have to tell my mum something." Then he turned to Charlie again. "I don't believe this is happening. Was that really me said I'd help?"

Charlie went first, slithering across to the pram with the torch. But then he stopped and flashed it about. "That's odd," he said. "I left it right here. What's it doing over there?" He shone the beam along the hedge. There stood Ma Perkins's pram, all black and lonely in the foggy light. He walked over and lifted back the straw bale so Wayne could take a look. Inside, sitting up all comfy, very much like Biddy must have done once upon a time, was a large badger with its eyes shut.

"Batty 'alfpints," Wayne breathed. "Where did you get that?"

Charlie hadn't answered. Wayne had to look round for him. He found Charlie down on the snow flashing his torch around.

"I got the idea once I worked out they were all being wasted," he said, when he'd got up. "The ministry men were just leaving them down in their holes. Here, you know those shoes Dave Cork had. Well, take a look at these. They're never badgers"

He shone the light down on the snow for Wayne to see. Their own footprints had been stamped into the snow all round the back of the pram, but round the sides there were a whole lot more, like some animal had been dancing about. Charlie lifted his torch. They were everywhere. Two long trails of paw prints, great wide deep things, led off into the dark.

"So how did this lot get here?" Charlie's voice

went suddenly sharp. "It was all smooth snow when I arrived. I lit it up with the torch. This lot's come since I've been here!"

Wayne looked where Charlie's torch was pointing. Whatever had made its mark down there in the snow didn't just have big feet. It had claws, long and thick, so sharp they had dug up green grass from below the snow.

"That's never dog prints," Wayne said. "That's never dogs'. Not even Meatloaf's got feet like that."

"It's not Meatloaf's," Charlie said. "I know it's not him." He straightened up and shone the light at Wayne, then he turned it on the prints at their feet. His voice dropped to a whisper. "So whose are they?"

Chapter Nine

When Charlie came crunching up the lane to school next morning, Wayne went skipping across the green to catch him before he got in through the gate. Charlie had his head down inside his own private fog and he kept going while Wayne trotted beside him getting his message out.

"You must have heard its dee-dah going," Wayne said when they got in through to the playground. "Everybody down here did. My dad went up to lend a hand."

Charlie just shook his head. "Must have slept right through it," he said, all casual like he always turned out to watch fires, but just for this once he'd decided to give it a miss. "What got burnt then?"

"That shed up the back where old Braddon brings on his geese, the one the ministry men have put all their stuff in. The firemen were saying they couldn't make out why it caught light. Someone had stacked a whole pile of straw and stuff all round it and set it on fire."

"Did all that ministry stuff get burnt then?"

"Dad said it would have poisoned all of us if it

had gone up too," Wayne said. "Pity you missed it."

Charlie shook his head again like he was sorry too. "Never heard a thing," he said.

Everybody was still shoving round in the corridor when Mr Greysock called out it was special assembly, straight in. Charlie had gone off round to Mr Flint's hole to see it there was any tea left. Martha Downs had to bring him back in.

Mrs Trugg was already up on the platform behind her bookstand. "No use your hiding down there, Charlie Coppins," she called, once Charlie had slid into his place. "I want you up here by me. Come along. We haven't got all day to waste."

Charlie's head really flicked up at that. Most times when he got called up on to the platform, he clumped off like it was no surprise at all, but this time he turned round to make sure it meant him and not someone else behind him.

"Stand right here, boy," Mrs Trugg said, all hard and gritty once Charlie was up there. She reached her right hand out for Charlie's arm and took it in her bone-breaking hold. People said they'd seen Mrs Trugg straighten railings with her right hand, just by taking hold and shutting her eyes.

"Last night, children," she called out, spitting her words out so they bounced off the back wall, "this boy was seen, by a good friend of mine, OUT IN THE DARK!"

She stopped there for a little moment to make sure all her words had sunk in. She hadn't let go of Charlie.

"Out in the the dark. ON HIS OWN! Out in the dark, on his own, when he had been told TIME AND TIME AGAIN to go straight home. To go straight home the very moment he left school. Told. Clearly. IN THIS VERY BUILDING!"

She didn't look at anyone after that. Instead, she stared straight up into the roof, as though the very sight of Charlie would make the rest of her hair fall down.

"Well?"

Charlie was gazing politely at the floor but he should have been ready for it. Mrs Trugg suddenly shot her right arm out sideways, and since it was the arm holding Charlie, he went with it. Then she whipped it straight back in again, and most of Charlie came back in too. It was just his head came in a bit slower than the rest. It all looked dead painful.

"You can own up with the truth, Dreadful Boy," Mrs Trugg called up to the roof. "You can tell all these decent girls and boys just what you were doing, out there in the dark when you'd been told. Well?"

She shot her arm out again for another great

lunging shove, but this time Charlie was ready for her. He came up on his toes and skipped off sideways, and then nipped smartly back in again. It saved his head coming off, but Mrs Trugg didn't let go.

"I was taking Mrs Perkins's pram back for her," Charlie answered, all loud and clear for the people at the back. "She'd lent it to my mum and I was taking it back."

"With a bale of straw on top?" Mrs Trugg called up to the roof. "Mrs Perkins had been so kind as to lend your mother a bale of straw?"

Charlie flew off again in another lunging shove.

"It wasn't Farmer Braddon's straw, it was my dad's," Charlie called out, trying to keep his dignity while he took off dancing sideways again.

Mrs Trugg whipped her glasses off with her other hand and smiled her grateful smile she kept for special times like when she reckoned the truth had been well and truly got at.

"And why has this Dreadful boy mentioned Farmer Braddon's straw," she called down to the rest of the hall. "Did anyone hear me mention Farmer Braddon's straw?"

Everyone shook their heads of course. People who didn't shake their heads at times like that knew they'd get shown up straight off that they were on the wrong side.

"Well I never done none of it," Charlie

suddenly shouted. Mr Flint's just told me it was Farmer Braddon's straw got set on fire, that's all and it wasn't me. That was my dad's straw I'd got. Ask anyone."

"It's Sergeant Edgely I'll be asking, Dreadful Boy," Mrs Trugg shouted back. "I'll be asking him to take you away and lock you up where all wild and reckless people deserve to be locked up for burning down other people's barns. Wild and reckless, that's what you are. Mr Greysock, will you come up here please and take this boy away until Sergeant Edgely comes for him. Upsetting all the children like this." She shoved her glasses back on to get a better look at everybody else, but it brought the rest of her hair down instead. Another special assembly was over.

Back in the classroom no one said anything. Charlie looked that wild even Daryl Manners kept his head down. Mr Greysock came back in and gave work out for people to do just like nothing had happened, but it was plain to see he was keeping his eye on Charlie. Once everybody had been given something to get on with, he sat down at his table and called Charlie out.

"You know someone tried to burn down the shed with the all the ministry men's stuff last night, don't you," he said quietly to Charlie. "You didn't really have anything to do with it, did you."

Charlie took his time coming back with an answer, and when he did, it came back all gulpy and jerky. "Everybody round here's always so quick and ready to tell on people," he said. "They're always blaming the wrong people for things they've never done. I never done any of all that, and straight off Mrs Trugg says it's me. Everybody does that round here. They done it on me. They done it on Meatloaf. People just go round mucking things up like they've got nothing better to do." He stopped just there, like he found it hard going on. Then he said his last bit. "If people had left my dad alone, he'd still be here."

He put his arm up over his face and hunched up his shoulders, fishing in his jeans pocket with his other hand.

Mr Greysock gave him a tissue. "Go on back to your chair, Charlie," he said. "I'll have a word with Mrs Trugg. We don't need Sergeant Edgely."

It was embarrassing seeing Charlie Coppins get so fussed, out there in front of everybody. If Mr Greysock had called Charlie out and had another go at him like Mrs Trugg, Charlie wouldn't have cracked like he did. It never helps when people start being kind.

Most people stayed staring at their work when Mr Greysock looked up. Daryl Manners had been grinning across at Andy Timms, but he wasn't that stupid to keep it up once Mr Greysock was looking at him. Moira Flynn had been muttering to herself right through Charlie's talk to Mr Greysock like she wanted to get up and say something herself, but Martha Downs kept pulling her back into her chair again. Trust Moira Flynn to have something to get up and talk about at a time like that.

At playtime, Charlie and Wayne went off round to the fan hole. Colin Dibble went out to see how Charlie was, but everybody else stayed inside in the warm. Even when the ministry men went past the window nobody rushed over for a stare. The only one to say anything was Andy Timms.

"Spacemen come to collect Charlie Coppins," he announced. "Is he all packed and ready for his trip to the moon?"

"Don't think he'd like to leave Biddy's pram behind," Daryl Manners called back. "Perhaps they'll let him take off in that. You going with him, Bid?"

Biddy was on the floor in the reading corner so she didn't hear. Mr Greysock did, but oddly enough, he didn't say anything. He was leaning back in his chair, watching Martha Downs and Moira Flynn through the steam off his tea. There wasn't much Mr Greysock missed.

* * *

After play, Mr Greysock decided to brighten things up by getting everybody to do something different. He shoved his tables book back in his drawer and went over to the cupboard.

"Something different this morning," he announced. "Those Nature Trail posters have come. You remember, the ones with the footprints on? Dave, if you've come to school in those paw mark shoes of yours, you can print them on a piece of paper and we can see if they match the ones on the posters."

He reached into the cupboard and pulled out a roll of posters wrapped up in brown paper. "Biddy and Damian," he said, "help me dish them out would you. There's enough for one each. Now, choose any animal off the poster that grabs your fancy and draw it in your nature books. Make sure you get the right paw marks and put them on the page too. We can do a project and put it up on the wall for visitors." He sounded very bright about it all.

There were footprints on those posters for just about every animal that ever had feet. Everybody showed off they knew all about dogs' feet and cats' feet, of course, but when it came to really wild animals nobody knew anything.

Charlie was leaning over his poster and not saying a word. Wayne looked across to see what he thought about it all, but Charlie hadn't noticed.

He'd got his pencil out and started drawing. Then he took his ruler out of his desk and laid it on the poster like he was measuring the paw marks and setting them down on his nature book page. Even when the dinner bell went he still had his head down. Most times, Charlie was the first one out through the door the moment the dinner ladies rattled their buckets.

"Charlie, we're going on with it this afternoon," Mr Greysock called over. "There'll be plenty of time to get it done. Everybody's gone in for dinner. Off you go."

Wayne slipped out round to the fan hole once he'd finished his pudding, but Charlie wasn't

there. He went across to the toilets and rattled all the doors. Lots of people yelled back, but Charlie wasn't there either. Wayne found him back in the classroom, sliding his ruler over his poster page, measuring footprints.

"What are you doing here?" Wayne asked, all mystified, like he'd caught Charlie doing something really odd. "The whistle's not gone yet. Come on out. It's dead boring in here."

Charlie shook his head. "I've got all this lot to check out yet," he said. Then he sat back and let his breath slide slowly out through his nose. "You know what," he said. "There's something here that just doesn't add up."

"*You* don't add up, if you ask me," Wayne answered. "There's hours of dinner play still left and you're in here creeping round old Greasy getting your work done. You've got the rest of today for all that."

"I haven't," Charlie answered. "I'm doing my sewing with Miss Tinsdale this afternoon, aren't I. She's brought in some old leather gloves she's got, so I can practise cutting them up. She's got some special scissors for it."

"Are you really going on with all that?" Wayne asked. "And just where's that smelly old corpse anyway? I bet it stinks your dad's workshop out. Badgers honk bad enough when they're fit and well. I reckon that thing's gone off that bad it must be just about ready to push the walls out."

"It's not up at the workshop," Charlie said. "It got stuck so bad I brought it on down again. It's still in Ma Perkins's pram. I've shoved it in the back of her barn."

Wayne stared. "Ma Perkins's barn?" he said. "In her pram? You know it's late night shopping tomorrow. She takes that pram down for late night shopping. She always does. You've not left yourself much time!"

Charlie just smiled his spit-in-the-wind smile like he had it all planned, thank you. "No problem," he said. "I'm taking it up after school. My leather business starts up tonight. I can take your order now if you want. There'll be shaving brushes, leather purses, watch straps, you name it and the Coppins Leather Works will make it. You can come up and watch the very first sweep of the craftsman's knife if you want."

As it turned out, Charlie's first sewing lesson never got anywhere. He had only just got settled in a corner with Miss Tinsdale's special scissors and her old gloves when Mrs Trugg came bursting in.

"So sorry to interrupt your lesson before it's begun, children," she called, just like Mr Greysock with all his cardboard book bits and Miss Tinsdale and her wool basket weren't there. "Sergeant Edgely has come for a quick word.

Now, settle just where you are, and listen carefully, please, and politely to what he has to say."

"I'll be very quick, everybody," Sergeant Edgely said. "I've come in specially to tell you just this. We've had a sighting of an unidentified creature out along Pitchy Ridge. I think we're close to the end of our search."

Everybody had to turn round for a stare at Biddy Perkins, of course, but she had turned round too, and she was staring back at Charlie Coppins. It was Charlie who looked like the one who'd had the shock. He'd gone all hot and red, and he'd hunched up in his corner like it was time to jump through the window.

"Now this is the important bit," Sergeant Edgely said. "I'm bringing in a special team of marksmen from the Castlebury police station. Farmer Braddon is going to help us too, seeing he knows the lie of the land better than any of us. Mrs Trugg has kindly agreed for you all to go home early, just today, to make sure you are all out of harm's way. No one, absolutely no one, is to stay outside their doors till me and my team come down and tell you it's all over. There's going to be guns and bullets and sniffer dogs out there in the dark, and all of us very busy. Is that quite clear?"

That really set up a buzz. Mrs Trugg clapped her hands just to get heard. "You all know what you have to do, children," she called out over everybody's conversations. "Get your coats from the corridor, and straight off home."

But then she let out a squawk like she'd just got trodden on. "Who is that boy pushing through so rudely, Mr Greysock? Is that Charlie Coppins? Just you come back, Charlie Coppins and mind your manners. Did you hear?"

But Charlie was already half way down the corridor to the outside door. Wayne saw him pull it open, leaning over all hot and scowling like he wasn't stopping for anyone. For someone in such a tearing hurry, it was strange Charlie had managed to take anything with him. But he had. Tight in one hand was his paw mark poster.

Chapter Ten

"Well?" Wayne asked Charlie, the moment he got into school next morning. "Go on, tell us then. You went charging off last night with your backside on fire. You trod on Mrs Trugg. Did you know that? You're up to something, aren't you?"

Charlie stayed reading Mr Flint's paper. "Oh, that," he said, all airy. "I just had to tidy up a few things, that's all."

"Just tidy up things? You trod on Mrs Trugg! You must have heard her yell at you. She's told Mr Greysock she's going to get you for it, first thing. You ran off home, didn't you, just because Sergeant Edgely was coming round?"

Charlie shook his head. "He only went round down in the village after all that," he said. "Old Braddon had to go sniffing round too, of course. He was telling everybody he was going to smack that killer dog right off the map, but he didn't find nothing."

"You got Ma Perkins's pram back all right then?"

That really brought Charlie out from behind Mr Flint's paper. He leaped clean out of his chair and smacked his head like he'd got bees in it. "Oh no! Batty 'alfpints! I batty forgot, didn't I! I've not done it. Oh glory!"

Wayne scrambled out of his way. "You dumb bozo!" he hissed. "It's Thursday. She takes her pram down late night shopping, Thursdays. You're too late!"

Charlie smacked the table this time. "No I'm not, not if I get out right on the bell when it's going home time. I'll have to move though. I was that busy last night, I clean forgot."

"You said you only had to tidy things up," Wayne said. "It must have been a right old mess if it made you forget Ma Perkins's pram. I reckon you were doing a sight more than just tidying things up. Just what are you up to, Coppins?"

Charlie slid over to the door and pulled it shut. "I was going to tell you anyway," he whispered. "You've got to keep it to yourself, though. If it gets round I'll know who told."

"'Course I won't tell. Go on then."

"I've got Meatloaf. He's up over my workshop so they can't get him."

Wayne stared. "You've got Meatloaf? Up over your workshop? Have you gone clean off your steaming porridge-pot? Sergeant Edgely and old Braddon have been snooping round looking for him for days. They're going to kill you!"

"They'll never know. Biddy helped. Her mum thinks he's just gone off again. He's got a bed and all sorts up there. I reckon he's not going to want to leave even when it's all safe again."

"So why did you belt off like that? Meatloaf was all right, wasn't he?"

"It was Sergeant Edgely starting up about sniffer dogs. I take him out once it's dark so he can stretch his legs, but he's got some mucky habits, that dog. I had to get home quick just to shovel up round the yard and splash a bit of paraffin around. Those sniffer dogs would've been dead interested, else. Next time I take him for a walk, I'm going to soak his feet in something special just in case they come back for another sniff."

"But you can't keep Meatloaf for ever," Wayne said. "What about your mum finding out. What are you feeding him on anyway?"

"I'll tell you," Charlie said. "I've got – " But at that moment, Mr Flint came pushing in.

"Come on then, lads," he said. "Whistle's gone. They're all in. You won't be staying tonight, I suppose."

"Can't," Charlie said. "Got to get off home, like Mrs Trugg said. He looked over at Wayne. "I've got something to check up on anyway," he said. "And it really can't wait."

Bad news struck at dinner time. The dental caravan came trundling into the playground and parked under the staffroom window.

Everybody set up moaning and groaning, of course, but Mr Greysock told them to save their misery for someone else. He wasn't having his teeth done, that was quite clear.

"You ungrateful lot ought to be really glad there are grown-ups willing to give up their time and energy making sure your teeth aren't rotting in your heads," he said. "Just imagine if you were a wild animal, and you got toothache. They get all sorts of diseases out there, wild animals do. They don't have Nurse Toumy running round pumping medicine into them."

"They get Farmer Braddon running round pumping gas into them," Mary Scriven said, all sniffy.

"Yes, but that's for quite a different reason," Mr Greysock said. "It's a bit tough on the badgers though, all that."

"They really are killing them," Martha Downs called out. "My dad told me. It's real poison they're shoving down those badger holes. I think it's wicked."

"How did we get round to badgers again?" Mr Greysock asked. "I was telling you about the benefits of the dental service. Now – "

"It must be pretty heavy stuff, that badger mixture," Daryl Manners put in. "Why don't they spread some of it round for the killer dog? Save a lot of fuss, that would."

Everybody groaned at that. Manners could be really thick sometimes.

"And poison every living creature that so much as came round for a sniff?" Mr Greysock asked. "That would really save a lot of fuss. Now then, at three o'clock we're lining up in alphabetical order for the dentist. It's just a check-up. He'll send a note to your mums if he thinks you need to come back. That's if Daryl's planning to let us all live that long."

There was one person who hadn't said anything, even though Mr Greysock had been letting everybody get a word in. That person was still leaning over his drawing, like he was hard at work. What with all the talk about killer dogs and murdered badgers it would have been hard for anyone to have missed any of it, but Charlie Coppins didn't seem to have heard a word.

It's strange how some people never come to understand just how hard it is to have a conversation while the dentist is inside their mouths, busy with his pronger. Nurse Toumy tried it with Charlie. No sooner had Charlie slid up on to the dentist's chair and laid himself out flat when over she came for a chat.

"That's a nasty scratch you've got there on your neck, Charlie," she said, coming in close for a stare. "It looks quite inflamed. Has your mum seen it?"

"Haarg," Charlie answered, shaking his head very slowly to save getting stabbed by the pronger.

Nurse Toumy put her hand on Charlie's forehead. "You're really quite hot, dear. I hope you haven't got an infection. Once Mr Dunn's finished, I'll just pop a thermometer in under your tongue and see how you're cooking. We don't want you spreading germs round now, do we?" She bent over and took another look. "I'd have said they were claw marks. Dirty things, claws."

The dentist pulled his mirror out for a wipe. "I think I got it while I was carrying something," Charlie said carefully. "Perhaps it didn't realize it was scratching me. I'm sure it didn't mean to. Is that me done then?"

"Come over here then, dear. Open wide, that's it. Under your tongue."

Colin Dibble watched from the doorway. He was next in the line so he couldn't help hearing. He was never one to miss someone else's conversation, but he nearly fell through the door making sure he caught this one. Once he was finished he skipped out of the dental caravan to tell Wayne he'd wait for him till he was done too. Then they walked off across the green with their heads down so nobody could listen in.

"Nurse Toumy's found out Charlie's gone odd." Colin couldn't get his news out quick enough. "She felt his head first and then she saw his scratches and now he's got a temperature. That's why he's still in school. She's taking him home in her car so he can't spread his disease all round everywhere. That great long scratch is where the badger got him isn't it? It's all swollen and poisoned. And you know what he told her? He said it didn't know it was scratching him, like it hadn't done it on purpose. He didn't mention it was batty dead!"

"I tried to tell him. I really tried," Wayne was muttering. "He wouldn't listen though, would he, not Coppins!"

Dibble suddenly stopped in his tracks. "You don't really think he's spreading poison round, do you?" He suddenly blew all his air down through his nose like he was cleaning it on the snow. "Yer-yuk! It could've crawled right into me. I've been next to him all morning!"

"I told him," Wayne said again. "It's his own fault. It could be eating his brains out for all we know. I bet Nurse Toumy just thinks he's got flu or something."

"I'm going to tell!"

"Tell Nurse Toumy?" Wayne said. "You'd go off and tell Nurse Toumy? She'd trot round to Mrs Trugg straight off and blow the whole thing. Then what? We'd get dragged up for a public execution the moment we got in school. We've just got to hang on, that's all. For all we know, Charlie might really have got flu. No point in rushing round telling people if he really has."

Colin didn't answer straight off. In fact, when Wayne thought about it later, Colin didn't answer at all. Instead, something quite different happened that took his attention off Colin altogether. Out through the fog, on the other side of the green, someone let go a really wild scream. The wild scream had come out of Pearson's Stores.

"It's here!" Dibble took hold of Wayne's arm and shook it like he thought Wayne wasn't paying attention. "It's here! Listen!"

Wayne stopped, but Dibble kept going. He must have decided that Wayne would be able to hear things a lot better if he was on his own. Without even a good-bye, he took off through the snow and headed for home, making a wide loop round the edge to save getting in too close to the shop. All Wayne could do was watch him go. Then he stepped over to Pearson's Stores.

He got only as far as the phone box when Pearson's doors barged open, and a strange collection of people burst out into the fog. The first one out was Ma Perkins, backwards, pulling her pram. Close behind, helping her shove it out and yelling all sorts by way of encouragement, was Mr Pearson.

"Get it out of here! Get it out!" That was the first bit of conversation Wayne was able to make out. Then Mr Pearson turned to call back into the shop. "Get the police, Milly. Get the police!"

Wayne slid over for a peep through the window, but finding a gap in the advertisements wasn't easy. What he saw, once he'd found a space, must have taken his breath away. The shop was empty. Everybody must have flocked out

behind Mr Pearson. What was left looked like they'd had a really wild party.

The great pyramid of baked beans he'd spent most of last Saturday stacking up to the ceiling had gone. Someone must have run right through it. The sheepskin slipper bin was full of toilet rolls. The alley up the middle looked like a trolley park caught in a hurricane where everybody had dropped everything and run. Mrs Pearson's till had its drawer open with all its money lying there like nobody wanted it.

Wayne stared. It all looked so silent and still. Outside, behind him, it was terrible. People were shouting and shoving and getting up to all sorts.

Ma Perkins was yelling louder than anyone. "How was I to know?" she was asking anyone looking her way. "I never saw the batty thing till I took me covers off. Someone's done a trick, that's what they've done. Don't you batty well shout at me. It's not my fault!" She went up close to Mr Pearson's ear. "Not my fault!"

Mr Pearson heard her all right, because straight off he took to shouting back. "Not your fault, woman? You've done this on purpose! Clear as day. The police will sort you out, you wicked woman. You and that mad dog of yours. Nothing but trouble the lot of you." He turned his back on her to shout into the shop. He couldn't have noticed that Mrs Pearson and all his customers were out there with him dancing in the snow. "Milly? Are they coming?"

What with all her practice at bringing the cows home for milking and Biddy home for tea, Mrs Perkins had grown a much bigger voice than Mr Pearson. "Wicked yerself!" she yelled back. "Ain't you batty listening? I never saw it, not till I got me covers off. Anyone would tip their pram over, getting a shock like that. Go on, ask them!"

But Mr Pearson didn't get a chance to ask anyone anything. A light came sweeping down the lane. It wasn't Sergeant Edgely's blue one. This was an orange one, shooting out stabs of orange light that twisted round and round on the top of the ministry men's landrover. Two men in white overalls jumped out, had a quick conversation with Mrs Pearson and pushed their way through into the shop.

What Wayne saw next sent him rolling back from the window and along the wall into the shadows.

The two men pulled on long orange gloves and bent down behind the slipper bin just like they were going to put it back on its legs. But they didn't.

Taking hold of either end, and leaning back to take the weight, they lifted something a lot heavier.

It was a very large, dead badger.

Chapter Eleven

It was the crowd standing round outside Pearson's Stores in the morning that brought Colin Dibble to a stop. He must have worked out straight off something was wrong. Pearson's was always open on his way to school, but today it was shut.

The blinds were down. There was a long piece of red ribbon stretching all the way across the windows, from the drain pipe by the side gates to the wrapper bin on the other side. And it all smelled odd. It smelled just as though Farmer Braddon had been round with his pig disinfectant. Dibble was still staring when Wayne Nuttley came out through the gates.

"They're not going to open all day," Wayne whispered, and he looked up over Colin's head like he was expecting Mrs Pearson to fling her window open for another yell. "They're not even doing the papers."

"What's happened then?" Colin whispered back. He wasn't whispering because he expected Mrs Pearson's window to fly open. He was whispering because his mouth had gone all dry with everything being so serious. "Why's every-body standing round? It's nearly whistle time."

"You don't know what's happened, do you. You missed it all. If you'd not gone off home you'd have seen it."

"Mum had visitors."

"Well you missed something," Wayne said. "It was Ma Perkins and her pram, all that screaming. She brought it down for late night shopping. The pram, dimmo!" He stopped and watched Colin so he wouldn't miss seeing him twitch.

Dibble twitched all right. He let go a sort of shriek too, like something fairly cross had just grabbed his bottom.

Wayne pulled him away so the others couldn't hear. "Don't you go giving things away," he hissed. "Charlie said he was going to clean it up but he couldn't, could he, not once Nurse Toumy took him off home. Ma Perkins didn't know she had a passenger till she took the covers off. She went right into the shop with it. That's what all the screaming was about. She got such a fright when she saw what she'd got, she tipped it right out on the floor."

"Who's got Charlie then?" Colin whispered.

"Charlie? Nobody's got him. He's up home. I don't reckon he knows anything's gone wrong. I'm waiting here so I can tell him."

"Well it's nothing to do with me!" Colin's

132

whisper turned into a squeak. Dibble always squeaked when he got excited. "I never touched nothing. It's Coppins got himself poisoned, not me. There's no one can say it's me!" He started hopping round like he wasn't sure which way to walk next. "It wasn't me! I went straight off home like Mrs Trugg said!"

He was still hopping about when Damian Tullet came over. "D'you know what?" Damian said. "Ma Perkins has gone clean off her porridge pot this time. She went in Pearson's and slung a dead badger on the floor, just so they'd have to close down. She's been took off in the ministry men's truck. They reckon they'll have to burn Pearson's down now, just so they can kill the germs."

Marlene Toms joined in. "My dad heard Farmer Braddon saying it's been Ma Perkins all along. That's why she's been letting Meatloaf off to go round killing things. He's going to get her locked up."

There was hardly anyone in the playground when the whistle went, they were all on the other side of the green watching the red ribbon dancing across the front of Pearson's blinds. "Watch out for Biddy!" someone called over. "She blew her bolts when they said it was Meatloaf. Wait till she finds out we know it was her mum!"

Oddly enough, there wasn't a special assembly.

Charlie came in from the caretaker's hole wiping Mr Flint's tea off his mouth, but he didn't look like he was expecting the roof to fall on his head. Wayne watched him. Most times, Charlie would have called over, but this time he just flopped down on his chair like he'd been out on the cross country course. Perhaps he really was expecting the roof to fall in and he was just trying not to let it show.

It was different when they got out round to the fan hole at playtime though. Wayne got his say in first, the moment they got round the corner.

"You've done it now, Coppins," he called. "You've gone and done it this time. I thought old Ma Perkins was a friend of yours!"

Charlie just looked blank. "What you on about nut-case," he said, getting in close to the fan smoke.

"What am I on about? I'm on about Ma Perkins and her pram, that's all! She tipped your smelly old corpse out on Pearson's floor, that's all!" You've been too busy planning your summer holiday to take it out, bozo! She's been dragged off by the ministry men for it. Farmer Braddon's going to get her locked up!"

Any other time Charlie would have jumped in and given Wayne a dead leg for all that shouting, but this time he just stood and stared. He stood there with his mouth so wide open his tonsils showed. Then he shut his mouth and swallowed.

"She said she was going out to Castlebury," he whispered. "She never said she was going shopping in Pearson's. She never did."

"Well, after all that creeping round the Perkins lot, being helpful, you've ended up getting her locked up. You really are very clever!"

Charlie didn't say anything else straight off. He just turned away like he wanted to get back inside. Then he leaned over and stared down into the drain where the washing up bits went. Then he was sick. It was a great, groaning, heaving sick like nothing wanted to come. Then it did.

Colin Dibble came hopping back in from having his dinner at home like he had something really new to tell. "Charlie's just gone off in a taxi," he called through. "He's just gone off in a taxi with his mum. I saw them out in the lane. Where's he going then?"

"He's been sick down the kitchen plug-hole and his mum's had to come home from work for him," Marlene Toms said. "He's got an infection."

Colin shoved straight through to Wayne's desk at that. "Infection? What's all that about Charlie's got an infection?" he asked, all anxious. "He was all right before dinner time."

"Well he's not all right now. He's heaved his guts up, hasn't he. Should have stayed home, I reckon, he looked that hot and wobbly. I told him he'd get it."

Colin really stared. "Get it? Get what? He's caught that badger disease hasn't he. Go on, he's got that disease. He caught it off that scratch he got. I'm going to tell!"

"Tell them what?" Daryl Manners called over. "What are you twittering on about, Dibble?"

"Nothing you need know," Wayne called back. "Charlie's got gut-rot, that's all."

"Oh no he hasn't!" Colin squeaked. "He's gone and got that badger disease. Nurse Toumy said he was all infected when he was having his dentist inspection. I heard her tell him. Charlie's been coming to school all this time since and he's been spreading his germs over all of us!"

"So how's he managed to get himself all diseased when nobody else has," Daryl said. "What's so special about Coppins?"

"Because he's a tacky little weasel," Marlene Toms got in. "Tacky little weasels catch all sorts, tacky little weasels do."

Colin looked at Daryl Manners, and then he looked back at Wayne again. "Go on then, Wayne," he said. "You tell them. It's true."

Wayne just went in behind his comic, like he wasn't telling anyone anything.

Colin took a deep breath. "He got it mucking about with a dead badger," he said, all loud and clear. "He got this dead badger so he could cut it up in handwork and make things to sell in Castlebury market." Then he stopped for a think, trying to work out if the next bit was worth saying. It was. "That badger Charlie got. It was the same one in Ma Perkins's pram. It was Charlie put it there."

That really got through. Not many people had been bothering with Dibble and his news till then, but that last little item caught just about everybody.

"What's that about Charlie?" Martha Downs came shoving through. "You said Charlie slung that dead badger in Pearson's?"

"He did an' all," Marlene Toms shouted over. "He hid it inside her pram so she'd be the one to take it in, instead of him. Isn't that just typical? And now he's gone and poisoned himself as well. Marvellous!"

"Serves him right," Moira Flynn called out. "He doesn't respect nothing, that Charlie. I bet he's crawling all over with bugs and fleas and poison mixture and nits and things. He just deserves to be sick. Makes me want to scratch just

137

thinking of it! Have you ever seen what a hedge-hog carries round with it? They're as big as – "

"Hang about!" Marlene Toms suddenly let go a shriek so wild it made everybody jump. "Think about it! All them crawly things Charlie's got. He's been all round us since then, breathing and dribbling and letting his steam out, and all that lot's been hopping off him every time he's moved. And just who've they been landing on? Come on, who's got them all now? Us lot! We've all got them now. Yer-yuk!" She jumped up on to her chair smacking her legs like they'd turned into spring-time carpets. "They're everywhere. We're all going to shrivel up and die!"

At that moment, Mr Greysock came stamping back from his dinner time stretch out. "I can hear you lot from right down in the staffroom," he said. "Marlene Toms, just what are you on about?"

"It was Charlie put that dead badger in Ma Perkins's pram, Mr Greysock," Marlene said, getting down off her chair. "Colin's just come in and told us. Charlie's got that badger poison off it. That's what's made him sick. Biddy's off sick too."

"We reckon Charlie's been spreading it round the whole school," Moira Flynn said. "We're all going to get it."

"Is this true, Colin?" Mr Greysock must have

thought it worthwhile asking or he wouldn't have bothered. "When did you hear this?"

Colin Dibble got up. "I only told, so that people would know what to give Charlie to make him better," he said.

Mr Greysock shook his head like he wasn't sure what to think next. "Well I'll be damned," he said. "If what you've told us is true, then we've got real trouble on our hands. I'm going up to Mrs Trugg's office to phone. All of you, get on with your projects – and I don't want to hear a word. Got that, Marlene? You've all enough to get on with. When I – "

But right then, someone else's voice took over, outside the window. Someone was shouting, out on the green. Mr Greysock went over to the window for a look. Everybody else came crowding in behind him.

It was Gramfy Blake. Out on the green. He was skipping across the snow and shouting out so loud it was like he didn't care if the whole village came out for a listen. Most times, Gramfy Blake went creeping round the hedges all quiet, catching rabbits with Mr Flint, but here he was, yelling his head off.

"I've seen it!" he was shouting. "I've seen it. It's up the old cottages. It's holed up in the old cottages. Get the police, Ken. Get the police!"

Mr Flint was already halfway over the green to

catch what Gramfy Blake was on about. Gramfy
grabbed his arm and pointed up to Railway
Cottages, then they both trotted over to the
phone box.

"That's up Charlie's house," Damian Tullet
whispered across. "That killer dog's in the old
cottages. Do you think they'll get it?"

"Old Braddon will," Andy Timms said. "He's
got his gun ready in the pick-up all the time so he
can be first there."

"Sit down, the lot of you. Moira, you're in
charge. Come on, move!" Mr Greysock really
shouted it. "Not a sound till I get back." And he
shoved out through the door, banging the playground door behind him.

"He's gone off to tell Sergeant Edgely, that's
where he's gone," Marlene Toms whispered
across to Moira. "They'll lob tear gas bombs in

and shoot it when it runs out. They always do that."

"A lot you know," Wayne Nuttley called back. "It's right next to Charlie's."

"Here," Martha Downs said. "It might be Charlie's window what Gramfy Blake was on about. It might have eaten Charlie already."

"Then it'll be dead with the badger disease before any of that lot get up there. Anyway, who said it was that hungry it wanted to eat someone like Coppins?" Daryl Manners got in. "It's not something I'd ever take on."

Marlene came back in with another hopeful thought. "Perhaps they'll have to burn down Charlie's house as well after all this. Isn't it getting exciting?"

But then Mr Greysock came back. "I've been talking to Mrs Trugg," he said. "We're all going home early. Now that means going home. Straight home. If I see any one of you hanging around in the cold there'll be trouble. Once the police team gets here, there'll be sniffer dogs and guns all around the place. Not one of you is to set foot outside your front door. Tell your mums and dads and aunties that's what Sergeant Edgely says. All understood? Yes, Martha?"

"My aunty's in London."

Mr Greysock closed his eyes for a moment like

he needed a quiet moment to himself. Then he let his breath slide out through his nose like he'd been counting. "You all know what to do," he said. "I'll be out there watching. I'm going home too, but I've got some visiting to do first. There's something going on here I can't quite make out."

Wayne Nuttley shoved out through the classroom door the moment the bell went. He was out through the gate and off up the path to Railway Cottages before Colin Dibble had even done up his buttons and got his gloves on. He was nearly out of sight by the time Mr Greysock shut the playground door quietly behind him. If Wayne had seen him come out he would certainly have stopped to watch, because Mr Greysock wasn't hurrying home like everybody else. He'd walked right past his car and over the green till he reached the bend past Pearson's. He'd gone to Biddy's.

Chapter Twelve

Charlie's front door was shut. Wayne shouted up at his window. Then he squeezed up a snowball and flung it up at the glass. He was so busy waking Charlie up he didn't notice Charlie coming round the corner from the back.

"Shush," Charlie whispered. "You'll scare it off!"

Wayne jumped. "I thought your mum sent you up to bed," he said. "You all right?"

"Mum's gone off to Castlebury. She said it was just something I ate."

"It wasn't," Wayne said. "Dibble's gone and told. You've got that badger disease. Old Greasy's told Nurse Toumy. They all know it was you put the badger in Ma Perkins's pram. They're coming out to lock you up."

But Charlie wasn't listening. He was standing there so hot and sweaty he looked like he'd just come in off the cross country race. Then he turned and stared out along the old railway line. "It's coming back for the chickens," he whispered. "It's just about time. I've got to be ready for it."

"What is?" Wayne said. "Are you all right, Charlie?" He looked out where Charlie was staring, just like a train was coming. "What are you on about, Charlie?"

"It's the thing with the other footprints," Charlie whispered. "Those ones by the pram. They're up here too. They're enormous."

"You've no time left for mucking about with footprints," Wayne said, all sharp. "Didn't you hear? They're coming to get you. They're coming to get Meatloaf too. Gramfy Blake's seen him. He's just come staggering into school and told Mr Flint. They know Meatloaf's up here, Charlie. Can't you get that?"

"Well, Meatloaf's got me looking after him now," Charlie answered. "No one's going to get him." He pulled back the shutter on his workshop door. "Listen, take him back down to Biddy's for me before they get here. Put him back in his old barn. They've been round that once. They won't go sniffing round a second time so soon. Once I've found that other one there's no one can hurt him." He looked so hot and anxious, when he turned to go inside he had to wipe his eyes with his sleeve to get the sweat out.

"But they'll bring sniffer dogs out." Wayne followed him up the stairs. "They're going to smell where's he's gone."

Meatloaf must have thought he was off to a party, even though Charlie was hanging round his neck croaking he was in for a bullet through his ears if he didn't hold still. He grinned over at Wayne with all his teeth out like he didn't have an enemy in the world. He was that happy with things, he didn't bother with all the odd things Charlie was doing. All Wayne could do was take over holding his collar, and watch.

Charlie was down on the floor pulling an old woolly sock up over one of Meatloaf's front paws. Then he fumbled round under Meatloaf's bed and came out with another one. When he'd finished, there stood Meatloaf with four woolly wellies on, right up to his knees. They were all different colours too, but Meatloaf didn't seem to mind. Charlie went over to the window sill and came back with an aerosol can. "Mind your nose, bozo," he said, and he carefully sprayed each of Meatloaf's feet. "It's my mum's," he said. "There's not many sniffer dogs going to want that lot up their nozzles."

Once he got out in the snow, Meatloaf went wild, of course. He danced about biting it like it was the top off his pudding, barking great happy barks they must have heard out in Castlebury. Then he took off down the path with Wayne leaping and flopping along behind him on his rope. Charlie watched them go.

*　*　*

Meatloaf took the quick way home. It didn't
bother him, because he was used to shoving
through hedge holes and clawing up banks, but
Wayne hadn't been that way before, not running
anyway. When he got back to the Perkins's yard
he must have reckoned Charlie owed him a
favour. Meatloaf never slowed up once. He kept
going right through the yard to their back door,
yo-yoing to be let in.

"Bid?" Wayne called, trying to shout in a
whisper so she'd come out quick and wrap Meatloaf up. "Bid? You in there? Open up, I've got
Meat – er, I've got a friend of yours. Come on
Bid, get it open!"

The bolts rattled on the other side. The door swung open. Meatloaf rocketted in through and Wayne stumbled in behind him. "Get the door shut quick," he hissed. "Get him out of sight. They're out looking for him!"

"And now it seems we've found him."

Wayne slammed to a halt, staring at the man in front of him. It was Biddy's house all right. It was Biddy's back door. This was Biddy's kitchen. This wasn't Biddy. Wayne suddenly needed the toilet. It was Mr Greysock.

"Come on through, Wayne Nuttley," Mr Greysock said. "I had a feeling somehow Meatloaf couldn't have vanished without a bit of help. Charlie Coppins is in this too somewhere, isn't he."

"He's gone off to find the real one," Wayne answered. "It's not Meatloaf, really it isn't, Mr Greysock. Charlie's found its footprints round his chicken house. It's a crew-cut dog. Charlie said. It's on his footprint poster."

"Charlie's gone off? In this?" Mr Greysock turned and stared out of the window. "Charlie's ill! I'm just about to go up there and talk to his mother!"

"But there won't be anybody there," Wayne said. "Charlie's mum's gone off to Castlebury and Charlie's gone after those footprints. He said he's got to find it before the hit squad get Meatloaf."

"He showed you on his poster, Wayne?" Mr Greysock sounded real sharp. "Can you remember which one it was? Think. It might be important."

"I've got mine upstairs if you want," Biddy said. She'd been down on the floor all this time singing greetings into Meatloaf's left ear flap. "It's on my door."

"Get it, Biddy, quick as you can." Mr Greysock went back to the window. It was snowing that thick it was hard to see across to the gate. "Charlie can't be out in this," he said to himself. "He can't be!"

Biddy came rustling back in through the door

and spread her poster on the table. "Charlie put a ring round it so I'd know if it came down here," she said. She got up on a chair and stared down at the pictures. Then she put her finger on the bottom corner. "That's the one," she said. "That's what Charlie's gone after."

Even in the dim of Biddy's kitchen the pencil circle Charlie had drawn showed up. Mr Greysock leaned over for a stare. Then he suddenly stepped back. "I don't believe it," he breathed. 'He's got it wrong. It can't be!"

Wayne took a look. "That's the one," he said. "That's its paw marks too. I've seen them." He squinted down at the print. "It's what I said. It's a cougar."

"But it can't be! Cougars don't live in England. They're savage great things living out in the wild. The only time you'd see a cougar in this country would be in a zoo or a wild life p – " and he stopped. "Oh no," he whispered. "It can't be!"

Wayne looked up at Mr Greysock, he'd stopped so sudden. Mr Greysock was staring down at Biddy's poster like he'd just thought of something terrible. "Wayne," he said, all sharp again, "get over to the phone box and dial 999. Just say you want the police in Castlebury. Tell them Sergeant Edgely's got to come out straight away. He might already be on his way but I don't know. Then get over to Farmer Braddon and tell him to get on up to Railway Cottages. Tell him he mustn't shoot. There's something up there all right, but Charlie's out there too. Tell him. Whatever he does, he mustn't shoot!"

Anyone passing Biddy's yard would have wondered what was going on right then. Wayne Nuttley came skipping out through the gates like he had bees in his hair. He whipped round the corner and pumped off down to the green. Mr Greysock came slithering out behind him, only he turned the other way, his collar up and his head down. In seconds they had both disappeared through the whirling snowflakes. Neither of them looked around. They were too busy watching where they put their feet. If they had, things might have been different. They didn't see the dark line of men moving carefully across the hill, each one turning carefully from one side to the other, watching every hollow and every hedge, working their way up to the old railway line like men who knew what they were looking for.

The telephone lady was dead sniffy about carrying messages about for people. She told Wayne he'd better not be mucking about or she'd tell the police to come round for him instead. Wayne skipped across into Farmer Braddon's yard after that, but there was nobody about. It was only when he turned the corner by the milking parlour he found out why. Standing by the combine shed was a dark blue mini-bus, its blue light on the roof nearly under the snow. It was the hit squad's bus. He was too late. The hunt had begun.

Mr Greysock found the sign for Charlie's footpath all right, but once he left the road, the snow got so deep it was like trying to run through water. He had to lift his foot out of the holes he was making just to make the next ones even deeper. He could hardly see anywhere in front. He was puffing so hard he had to stop and breathe quieter just so he could listen. Then he took to leaping and puffing again. He'd never been that way before, not even in summer time. There were trees getting in his way, and bramble thickets and sudden drops into hollows. He'd lost the path. He never heard the shout from over on the hill. If he had, he'd have dropped flat sooner.

"That's it!"

Someone far away to one side shouted. A gun cracked, once. Then it all went terribly quiet.

Chapter Thirteen

Wayne heard the bang, but he didn't stop to work out where it came from. He just turned and ran, out of Braddon's yard, back over the green and up the lane till he got to the start of Charlie's path. He never noticed Mr Greysock's trail wandering somewhere else, he just plunged on, skipping high out of his snow holes, like the path underneath had got too hot for his toes to stay with. The cold air hurt the back of his throat as he sucked it in and he could feel his dribble going icy while it slid down his chin, but he didn't stop to wipe it off. There wasn't time.

But then he did stop. He hadn't really reckoned on pulling up till he got all the way to Charlie's back door, but what came next really brought him to a slithering halt. Up ahead, something screamed.

Wayne listened, but it wasn't easy to work out. For one thing his heart was pumping so loud he couldn't hear much else, and for another, Charlie didn't scream that often, not like he was being killed, so it could have been anyone. It was more like a chicken anyway, the kind of scream they let go once they realize they're wanted for dinner.

Then a door took up slamming, like it had people on either side trying to win which way it had to go. Someone started shouting while it slammed.

"Get your batty foot out the way, will you? Leave off pushing! What else do you want, you've got your tea in there with you! Can't you hear it? Get – your – foot – in!"

Wayne ran on, skipping from tree to tree. Then he saw Charlie.

Mr Greysock heard the shot, even though he was puffing and grunting and stumbling about in the snow. At first, he thought he'd stop just where he was and think about it, but when the shotgun pellets came rattling through the brambles round his head he pulled his hat down over his ears and flung himself flat in the snow to work things out down there instead.

"Don't shoot!" he yelled into his hat. "You've got the wrong animal!"

Then he heard people calling. "I said wait till I gave the word, didn't I?" someone yelled over. "You're just too twitchy, you are. Always in a hurry. One day you're going to kill somebody!"

Mr Greysock lay there, listening through his hat. The brambles rustled around him. "There now," said a voice. "Didn't I just say? You come

153

over here and see what you've gone and done, Duncan. You've shot that nice Mr Greysock!"

It was time to sit up

Charlie was shoving against his chicken house door as if he badly wanted to keep it shut. "Stay in, won't you?" he was sobbing. "You'll be all right. Get your paw in and eat your tea. Please."

"Charlie? You all right?" Wayne ran across.

"Give us a hand, quick," Charlie shouted over his shoulder. "It's come in, but it doesn't want to stay. It's trying to – " and then the squawking stopped. Charlie shoved the bolt across. Then he went round to the window bars. "I knew you'd be hungry," he said.

"Hungry?" Wayne asked. "What's hungry?" He stepped over and looked down Charlie's torch beam.

Wayne told everybody about it afterwards, but of course he'd got over it by then. He never told people about his own squawk though, not the one he let go once he realized what he was staring at. He leaped away from the bars and dropped the torch, flinging his arms round Charlie like he was drowning.

"It's in there! It's really in there!" he yelled.

"It's got a chicken. We've got to get away!" He grabbed hold of Charlie and pulled him away. "It's seen us!"

But then a man's voice shouted up from the line. "Hullo? Is that you up there, Charlie? Are you all right? Over there by the trees, Sergeant. I heard voices!"

Charlie stayed in close to Wayne. "Didn't I say it never wasn't Meatloaf?" he whispered. "I knew it would come. I waited and waited."

Charlie's whisper was turning into a croak. "I've been waiting and waiting," he said again. "It's very hot out here." Then he slid quietly down into a heap on the snow.

"Charlie?" Wayne fell on his knees beside him. "Charlie? What you mucking about down there for? Charlie?"

Quite suddenly the yard started filling up with people. A line of men came shuffling in through the trees. More dark shadows trudged up from the line, crowding in round Charlie's chicken house. Arms reached over and lifted Charlie back up on his feet. Then a car came crunching in off the lane, lighting everyone up in yellow smoke. People were shouting, slamming doors, flashing their torches about. Wayne watched it all like he didn't belong. Then someone was helping him up and talking in his ear. It was Mr Greysock.

"It's all over, Wayne. It's all over," he was

saying. "They've taken Charlie into his house. Nurse Toumy's brought his mum back. This is terrible. He's lucky he didn't die out here."

"He's died indoors?"

"Charlie? No, Charlie's all right. He just about froze himself to death out here, but he's all right. Nurse Toumy says he's got the flu. Come on into the warm. He's asking where you've got to. Just imagine if his crazy plan went wrong. That cougar could have done for him. It really could. Gives me the shivers just thinking about it. Come on over and take a look."

Wayne followed Mr Greysock back to the window bars and then looked in again, back down the torch beam. There it was, a huge golden cat.

"It's a cougar," Mr Greysock whispered. "Just look at the size of it."

It was lying right across the chicken house floor from corner to corner. Its tail was pushed up tight against one wall and its great front paws were holding down a heap of feathery bones on the other. It was quietly growling to itself, licking round inside the last bits like it was cleaning out the cake bowl. It suddenly turned its head when the light caught it, and it flattened its ears and hissed, glaring its own eyes back up the torch beam like two red searchlights of its own. Wayne got down.

"It's all right. It's safe in there," Mr Greysock

whispered. "They're taking it home in the morning."

"Home? Has it got a home then?"

"It certainly has. They thought it had been burned to death in the fire, but it must have got out in time and made a run for it. No wonder they didn't find anything when they went scratching around in the ashes. It was bouncing around the moors looking for its dinner. I reckon they'll take better care this time."

Charlie stayed off school till he was better. People always look so clean when they come back after being away ill, but Charlie looked specially different. He came in through the playground gate in a new anorak. It was bright orange with a fur hood and zips on all the pockets to keep the weather out. It didn't really look like Charlie.

He just walked in like he hadn't been away. Daryl Manners and Andy Timms had a whisper, of course, but nobody else did much. Mr Greysock gave him a wink when he came out to blow the whistle, but he didn't seem surprised to see him.

Charlie got a surprise though, when he saw what everybody had done in their art lesson while he'd been off. Upon the walls there were leopards and cougars and tigers and all sorts. Some of them had their paws poking out through Charlie's chicken house door, with Charlie shoving up hard the other side trying to keep it shut. They were all staring at him through their stripes and spots, and all of them were growling and spitting like they'd be only too pleased to put their teeth into anyone if they cared to get up close.

There was just one up in the special place next to the Queen. Straight off Charlie knew it was Biddy's. Mr Greysock was always trying to get Biddy to use all her colours, but Biddy always chose black. There it was, a great black shape sitting outside Biddy's black house. It had all its teeth hanging out in a great wide smile like all the world had just been round and become its friend again. It was Meatloaf.

That was Charlie's first surprise. Soon after that he got a visitor. Mr Greysock brought him right into the classroom. Nobody knew who it was at first, but Charlie did. It was the lorry driver from the wild life park. He'd brought Charlie an invitation saying he could spend a whole day there for nothing and he could bring a friend if he wanted.

Charlie looked really embarrassed by it all. He had to come out and shake hands and take his invitation back to his desk with him, but it was plain to everyone he was dead proud they'd taken the trouble. Even Marlene Toms was clapping when he sat down.

He told Wayne Nuttley afterwards what he was going to do with it, when they got round to the fan hole. Colin Dibble was there too. Charlie had worked it out, and even Dibble understood. He was going to take it home and save it till later, for when he could take his dad.

Things got better after that. When Biddy's dad came out of hospital he still had to walk round with special crutches, so they told him he could come back inside the Lime Kiln if he wanted, and sit quiet by the fire. They never did burn Pearson's down. Mrs Pearson must have been thankful things never got worse, and she took to getting up from her till and helping Mrs Perkins with her shopping when she came in on late nights.

Nobody was sorry when the ministry men packed up and left. Farmer Braddon went round telling everybody they'd only slipped off home so they could work out better ways of doing things, but Moira Flynn said they'd gone because they were ashamed of all the unhappiness they'd caused. When she got up in class to have her say, Mr Greysock let her go on and didn't chip in with thoughts of his own anywhere. Moira was quite sure about it all. People ought to stop and think before they rushed in and put the blame in the wrong place.

Everybody had something to say, of course. Mr Greysock joined in when they'd all finished. He said Moira was quite right, but somebody else had thought up the idea ahead of her. A long time ago, he said. The trouble was, it had never really caught on. If it had, then a certain friend of Biddy Perkins would never have needed to skip round the countryside with funny socks up his legs, and his own precious hat would not now be letting the wind in. Trust Mr Greysock to come up with something that had nothing to do with it.

The only one not having a say was Charlie Coppins. He'd come skipping into school that morning with a letter from the postman, but Mr Greysock was the only one he'd shown it to. He was out in the shed, pulling out all the bits he'd need for handwork.

He wasn't doing sewing any more. Charlie was making a surfboard.